"I'd hoped it wouldn't become widespread knowledge that you were visiting the islands," Linc said, handing her the newspaper.

Maddie read the article, choking back a frightened cry.

"Maybe that's the man who's been s-stalking me," she stammered. "I thought he was watching me at the national park, too, but I didn't tell you because that person turned out to be a woman. I suppose I just imagined that she looked like the man."

Linc turned the page and pointed to the picture of the escaped criminal. "Does this look like the man you've seen?"

"Maybe, but I don't know. I've just had a few fleeting looks at him. Do you think I'm in danger?"

"I hope not, but perhaps you'd better go home. I want you to be safe."

Books by Irene Brand

Love Inspired

IRENE BRAND

Writing has been a lifelong interest of this author, who says that she started her first novel when she was eleven years old and hasn't finished it yet. However, since 1984 she's published thirty-two contemporary and historical novels and three nonfiction titles. She started writing professionally in 1977 after she completed her master's degree in history at Marshall University. Irene taught in secondary public schools for twenty-three years, but retired in 1989 to devote herself to writing.

Consistent involvement in the activities of her local church has been a source of inspiration for Irene's work. Traveling with her husband, Rod, to all fifty states and to thirty-two foreign countries has also inspired her writing. Irene is grateful to the many readers who have written to say that her inspiring stories and compelling portrayals of characters with strong faith have made a positive impression on their lives. You can write to her at P.O. Box 2770, Southside, WV 25187 or visit her Web site at www.irenebrand.com.

IRENE BRAND
YULETIDE
stalker

Steeple
Hill®

Published by Steeple Hill Books™

STEEPLE HILL BOOKS

Steeple
Hill®

ISBN-13: 978-0-373-87401-9
ISBN-10:   0-373-87401-4

YULETIDE STALKER

Copyright © 2006 by Irene Brand

This edition published by arrangement with Steeple Hill Books.

www.SteepleHill.com

Printed in U.S.A.

"And she brought forth her firstborn son, and wrapped him in swaddling clothes, and laid him in a manger; because there was no room for them in the inn."

—*Luke* 2:7

Thanks to our friend, Heryl Turner,
for providing basic research for this book by
taking me for a ride in his Cessna 172 Skyhawk.

ONE

The first twenty years of Maddie Horton's life seemed of little importance as she anticipated the next few weeks. This upcoming Christmas vacation promised to be a time of pleasure and adventure. Her first airplane ride. Her first trip outside the continental United States. And when she landed in Honolulu in a few hours, she would see Lincoln Carey for the first time in over ten years.

Recalling that momentous occasion when Lincoln, who preferred to be called Linc, came into her life, brought fleeting sadness to Maddie. Her father, Commander Stanley Horton of the U. S. Navy, had been on a six-month assignment to Hawaii when he was killed in an airplane crash Maddie was only ten years old. Linc, a junior officer under her father's command, had accompanied his body home to West Virginia for burial.

Unaware, the handsome sailor had stolen Maddie's impressionable heart at their first meeting. The years hadn't changed her affection for him. After her mother died, Maddie kept in touch with Linc with an occasional note. She had also sent him her high school graduation announcement, which he hadn't acknowledged.

But when she'd written to ask him to provide some information about Hawaii's role in World War II for a History project, he invited her to spend the Christmas holidays with him in Hawaii and do on-site research. Maddie had jumped at the chance to find out if the man she'd enshrined in her heart for ten years was as wonderful as she imagined.

Anticipating the trip, Maddie had become as flighty and excited as a kitten chasing sunbeams. She lived in a state of euphoria for weeks. But she'd come down to earth with a thud when she visited Caroline Renault, director of the Valley of Hope facility, where Maddie had lived for two years. VOH was a residence school for at-risk teenagers. Maddie didn't qualify for admission to the school for the usual reasons. But knowing that she was dying, Maddie's mother, who had been Miss Caroline's friend for years, had arranged for Maddie to live at VOH until she was eighteen.

"Did you seek God's guidance before you planned this trip?" Miss Caroline asked.

Embarrassed, Maddie admitted that she hadn't.

"I haven't received any positive reassurance when I've prayed about your trip," Miss Caroline continued. "Since you've already accepted the invitation, there isn't anything I can do except warn you to be careful. But I sense that danger waits for you in Hawaii."

Because she respected Miss Caroline and her opinions, her concern caused Maddie several anxious days. But in the excitement of the final preparations, Maddie often pushed her friend's cautionary words into the background. During today's ten-hour flight, though, she wondered if she *would* encounter some kind of trouble in Hawaii.

When she'd discussed her concerns with her roommate, Lucy Harrison, Lucy scoffed at the idea.

"What could happen, unless Lincoln Carey turns out to be a jerk?" Lucy said in her matter-of-fact way. "And you've got a return ticket. If he makes a pass at you, you can always go to a hotel for a few days. In the meantime, you'll have a lot of new experiences."

Her eyes sweeping Maddie from head to toe, Lucy asked, "Does Linc Carey know what you look like?"

"I've never sent him a picture. He probably remembers the way I looked when I was ten."

"And how old is he?"

"Eleven years older than I am. He's thirty-one now."

With twinkling eyes, Lucy said, "Chances are he still thinks of you as a child. Your appearance may be quite a shock to the man."

Remembering Lucy's lighthearted assessment of the situation eased Maddie's apprehension. She settled back in her seat and looked out the small window. When the plane took off from the Houston airport, she had been on pins and needles watching the rapidly receding ground. Below her now was a white layer of clouds. She took her Bible from her tote bag and searched for some Scriptures that dealt with clouds. One from the book of Isaiah resonated with her.

See, the Lord rides on a swift cloud.

Momentarily, she wondered if her feeling of being suspended in space was a foretaste of what Heaven would be like.

But another passage in Isaiah had always been special to Maddie since the day she'd accepted Jesus as her Savior and God as the Guide of her life.

I have swept away your offenses like a cloud, your sins like the morning mist.

The clouds blocked her view of Earth, yet they also served as a reminder of God's forgiving spirit.

Maddie put the Bible away and peered out the window again. Through occasional breaks in the clouds, she saw the wide sweep of the Pacific. She had chatted with the passenger seated to her left, a Hawaiian businessman, until he went to sleep during the movie. He was still sleeping. Fidgeting, eager to reach her destination, Maddie noticed a headline in the Honolulu newspaper on her companion's lap. Her eyes widened. She straightened in the seat while a flicker of apprehension tingled her spine. Leaning closer she read the headline.

Deathbed Confession Leads U.S. Navy to Investigate Ten-Year-Old Accident.

Her heartbeat accelerated. Maddie tapped the man gently on the shoulder. When he opened his eyes, she said, "May I look at your newspaper?"

Smiling, he handed it to her. "I've finished with it. Keep the paper, if you like."

Maddie gripped the newspaper in trembling fingers. Her hands moistened, and her rapid heartbeat threatened to choke her as she read.

Two inmates escaped from the federal prison yesterday. One of the inmates, Demitirio Sanale, was shot during the escape attempt. His brother, Kamu, is still at large. Demitirio died from his injuries, but on his deathbed, he confessed that he had been part of a plot that caused the death of a naval officer ten years ago. The airplane crash that took the officer's life had been considered an accident, but a new investigation into the crash has been launched. The public is warned that Kamu Sanale is armed and dangerous.

Maddie felt as if a hand was closing around her throat. Fearful images flashed in her mind. A dreadful flicker of uneasiness touched her heart. Could this incident be related to her father's death ten years ago? Maddie had accepted her father's death when she thought it was an accident in the line of duty as he served his country. But if he had been murdered, the old wounds would bleed again. Was this the reason Miss Caroline sensed she shouldn't go to Hawaii? Suddenly, Maddie wished she had never left home. But her troubled thoughts were interrupted when the pilot asked the attendants to prepare the cabin for landing.

As she always did when anxious, Maddie twisted the opal ring on her forefinger. Her father had given it to her mother as an engagement ring, and Maddie had worn it every day since her mother died. Once again, grief over her parents' untimely deaths engulfed her. She'd never felt so alone. Of course, Linc waited for her, but he was a stranger to her. Why had she been so foolish as to accept this invitation?

The attendants walked through the cabin collecting earphones, taking cups and other trash, while Maddie's heart pounded in anticipation coupled with fear. Following directions, she fastened her belt and restored her seat to an upright position. When she next glanced out the window, a sight of unbelievable beauty greeted her eyes.

The string of islands looked small in the vivid blue water. White waves pirouetted like mermaids in the surf. Volcanic peaks soared majestically toward the sky. There wasn't as much green as she'd expected, but she knew she couldn't compare this island paradise with the verdant forests of her native West Virginia.

As the giant plane dropped quietly toward the distant islands, Maddie tensed for the landing with a sense of unease. Would her vacation in Hawaii be as enjoyable as she'd imagined? She'd tried to put Miss Caroline's words out of her mind, but it was impossible to discredit what her mentor and friend had said.

Maddie had concluded that Miss Caroline thought it inappropriate for her to accept the invitation from a man she barely knew. Linc had assured her that he had a resident housekeeper as a chaperone, but she had only his word for it. After reading the newspaper article, Maddie feared that Miss Caroline's concerns heralded a more dangerous situation.

Wondering what he'd gotten himself into, Linc Carey nervously waited for Maddie's plane to land. He carried an orchid lei and the sweet scent of the blossoms stung his nostrils. When he starting pacing for the fifth time his companion, Ahonui Kingsbury, said, "Can't you sit still? The plane isn't due to land for fifteen minutes. I knew this would happen when you insisted on coming two hours early."

Linc sat down, but Ahonui's words annoyed him. In fact, her presence annoyed him. She had been his secretary since he'd organized his restaurant chain eight years ago. She didn't normally interfere in his private life, and he couldn't understand why she was so intent on coming to the airport with him. He was uncertain of how this visit with Maddie would turn out, and he didn't want anyone watching when he met the girl he hadn't seen for ten years.

"I don't know why you asked this child to visit

you for a whole month anyway," Ahonui said. "This is our busiest time of the year."

"She isn't a child. She's in college. And I invited Maddie for a visit because I promised her father I'd keep in contact with his family. I kept my commitment fairly well for a while, but I've been so busy the past few years that time got away from me."

Ahonui's perfectly curved eyebrow lifted as she asked, "Why haven't you mentioned her before this?"

Although he was tempted to say that he didn't see why it concerned her, he ignored the question.

"Maddie is researching Hawaii's involvement in World War II for one of her courses," he continued as he paced the short aisle where they sat, "and she asked me to send her some material on the subject. I realized that I hadn't kept in touch with Maddie and her mother as I should have, so I tried to make it up to her by inviting her to Hawaii during the semester break. While she's here, I'll take her to World War II sites."

"Well, I know she's going to be a nuisance to us," Ahonui countered.

Linc looked at her sharply. "*Us!* Maddie isn't your responsibility. I expect you to handle the office while I entertain her. I don't even know why you insisted on coming today."

"I'd think you would want me to help, especially now that you've finally realized she isn't a child."

He sat down again, but didn't bother to answer this comment. Roselina, his housekeeper, was all the help he needed in seeing that Maddie enjoyed herself.

When the arrival of the plane sounded over the loudspeaker, Linc jumped to his feet and walked briskly to the door where passengers would deplane from the security section. When he had talked to Maddie by phone two days ago, he'd asked, "How will I recognize you? I'm sure you've changed a lot in ten years."

"I'll wear my blue suit and a white shirt," Maddie had answered in a soft voice. "I have shoulder-length blond hair."

"Good. Then I'll have on a blue shirt with the Hawaiian flag on the pocket to help you find me," Linc had said.

His memory was hazy about Maddie's appearance. When he'd met her, he was burdened with the responsibility and grief of accompanying the body of his commanding officer. He remembered Maddie as a gangly child with vivid blue eyes and braces on her teeth. He knew very little about her teenage years because her letters to him, usually thank-you notes for gifts he'd sent, had been brief.

As Linc eagerly scanned the deplaning passengers, he sensed that Ahonui stood beside him. To add to his discomfort, many of the women unloading wore blue outfits, and he looked them over with increasing frustration. His surprise couldn't have been greater when a young woman paused before him, a half smile on her face.

"Are you Linc?"

Linc stared speechlessly at the vision of blond

loveliness looking up at him with the most beautiful eyes he'd ever seen. He'd grown accustomed to the dark features of native Hawaiians. Even people with light complexions spent so much time in the sun that it was unusual to see anyone with such fair skin.

His appreciative eyes swept over her facial features. Her dark blue eyes were framed by thick, curling lashes, a shade darker than the blond wavy hair tumbling over her shoulders. Her lips were full and rounded over even white teeth. A dainty nose was the focal point of a delicate face with a complexion blend of gold and ivory. Maddie had a petite, slender body. Linc had been expecting a girl, but Maddie Horton was a woman. He forgot about Ahonui standing beside him.

"Welcome to Hawaii, Maddie," he said huskily, and with hands that trembled he draped the lei over her head. As his hands rested momentarily on her shoulders, she stole a glance at his face.

Thick dark hair framed his classically handsome features. Clear gray eyes brimming with awe shone from a face bronzed by the sun. His mouth might have appeared stern if not tempered by the humorous quirking of his full lips. He towered almost a foot over her five feet three inches. Unnerved by her spinning pulses, Maddie looked away.

His mind reeling with confusion, Linc dropped his hands from her shoulders.

Ahonui's sarcastic voice sounded in his ear. "Aren't you going to introduce me?"

Suddenly, he was happy for her presence.

Shaking his head to clear it, Linc reached for the piece of luggage Maddie carried.

"Maddie Horton, this is my secretary and friend, Ahonui Kingsbury."

Maddie took Ahonui's hand, wondering at the speculative glint in the woman's eyes.

"Patience is my English name if you'd prefer to use that. You'll be seeing a lot of me."

"But I like Ahonui," Maddie said. "It's a pretty name."

"How was your flight?" Linc asked as he steered Maddie toward the luggage area. Ahonui took a place at Linc's other side.

"Since it was my first flight, I don't know whether it was typical or not," she said, and her eyes met his briefly. "But I enjoyed it very much. Thanks for making it possible for me to have this new experience."

"You'll be a flying pro before you go home. We do a lot of interisland flying here."

A piece of Maddie's luggage didn't arrive, and she assured Linc that she could manage without it.

"We'll report it to the claims department, and we can probably pick it up when we come into town tomorrow. I've set aside the day to take you on a tour of Honolulu."

When they reached the parking garage, Ahonui claimed the front seat of Linc's two-door car, leaving Maddie to climb into the back. Linc didn't like it, but he knew he couldn't do anything about Ahonui's behavior without making a scene that would embarrass Maddie.

As he left the airport, Linc spoke over his shoulder to Maddie, "We'll take Ahonui into town, then we'll head toward my home, which is ten miles from the city in the opposite direction. You've had a long trip, and you'll probably want to rest before we start sightseeing."

Linc soon pulled into the parking garage of a multistoried building and stopped near the elevator.

"My offices are on the tenth floor," he said to Maddie, "and I'll take you on a tour of them later." He left the car and opened the door for Ahonui.

"I probably won't be back to work for a week," he said to her, "but I'll check in by phone at least once a day."

Ahonui stepped out of the car, saying, "I hope you'll enjoy your visit in Hawaii, Maddie." Turning to Linc, she said quietly, "I just thought of something we need to discuss. Could I speak with you privately?"

Frowning, he said to Maddie, "I'll only be a few minutes." Linc followed Ahonui out of hearing.

"What's so important that it can't wait until tomorrow?" he asked impatiently.

"Do you think it's wise for you to be escorting that woman around these islands alone? I can easily go with you. The other secretaries can handle things until we're back."

Irritated more than he should have been, Linc

said, "I need a secretary this month more than I need a chaperone."

"How old is she anyway?"

"I don't remember her exact age, but I think she's twenty."

Laughing ironically, Ahonui stated, "She's the most mature twenty-year-old I've ever seen, and you're a bachelor. She might have designs on you. I'm just trying to protect her reputation...and *yours*," she added significantly.

He lifted his brows. "Surely I'm not such a rough character that my companionship would ruin anyone's reputation."

"That isn't what I mean and you know it."

Ahonui knew very well that he didn't date anyone steady, and she hadn't shown any interest in him, other than as her employer. He knew very little about her private life, so why was she so eager to follow him and Maddie around the islands?

"Let me worry about Maddie's reputation. You take care of the office."

Returning to the car, Linc opened the door and invited Maddie to sit in the front seat.

"I don't want to look like your chauffeur," he said with a grin. "Besides you can see better from up here."

Ahonui watched them leave, and Maddie wondered at the expression on her face. Was it fear that shone from her dark eyes? Or was she romantically interested in Linc? Since Linc had been her knight in shining armor for years, Maddie had hoped that her memory had remained in his heart, too. She supposed that Linc would always think of her as a child, and she knew she couldn't compete with Ahonui if Linc was dating her.

Ahonui was a tall, slender, almost excessively thin woman, but she walked gracefully, her well-shaped shoulders erect. She had heavy dark hair, olive skin and ebony eyes. Only a slight droop to her shapely mouth marred the beauty of her face. Her air of self-determination gnawed at Maddie's self-confidence. She had a feeling that Ahonui would stop at nothing to gain what she wanted.

Maddie's daydreams about the time she would spend with Linc had suffered a setback. Comparing herself to Ahonui, Maddie sensed that she came off second best. How close was the relationship between Ahonui and Linc?

TWO

Having noticed that many of the houses along the highway were small, unpretentious dwellings, the magnificence of Linc's home came as a big surprise to Maddie. After they left the main highway, for about a mile he guided his small red sports car along a private road lined with eucalyptus trees. They entered a sizable cleared area dominated by a two-story frame house with a steeply pitched roof. One striking feature of his home was a long, low veranda with sheltering eaves. A covered walkway connected the house to a nearby cottage.

Linc opened the car door for Maddie, and as she stepped out, she exclaimed, "Oh, it's beautiful. Is it a new house?"

Pleased at her response to his home, Linc shook his head. "It's a lot older than we are. This house was built in the thirties by the owner of a sugar plantation. After he died most of the land was snapped up by contractors who built resort hotels along the beach. But the woman who inherited the property didn't want her grandfather's home razed. I bought the house and four acres of land at a reasonable price. It was in bad condition, and it has cost a lot of money and hard work to renovate, but it was worth it."

"Oh, yes, I think so. And just feel that lovely breeze," Maddie said as the wind stirred tendrils of soft hair across her face.

"We're close to the ocean. Let me show you my favorite view."

He directed Maddie into a large living room furnished with overstuffed sofas and chairs. At the end facing the ocean, the wall consisted almost entirely of windows. Linc opened a sliding door onto a trellised porch that led to the ocean at the property's edge.

"My own private beach," he said.

Finding it hard to realize she was vacationing in such a wonderful spot, Maddie cried out, "I've come to paradise! What a fabulous place to live. No wonder you stayed here after you left the navy."

"Many people who move to Hawaii from the original forty-eight think it's too confining and soon return home. It's true that we're pretty much marooned from the rest of the states, but I've found everything I want here." Scanning Maddie's delicate, ethereal profile, he amended in his mind, "Or almost everything I've wanted."

"So there you are," a cheerful voice sounded behind them. "Mr. Linc, why didn't you bring the young lady to meet me?"

Maddie turned to see a short, chubby woman

standing on the veranda, hands on her hips. Linc motioned the woman toward them.

"Because I couldn't wait to show our guest the view. Maddie, this is Roselina Pukui—my housekeeper, friend and parole officer. If it wasn't for her, I'd get in all kinds of trouble."

Laughing at Linc's remarks, Roselina waddled toward them, her gentle black button eyes smiling.

"Don't pay no heed to him, honey." She wrapped her arms around Maddie, crushing the floral lei. The sweet scent of the orchids surrounded them. "Welcome to our home."

Even from her short stature, Maddie could look over the housekeeper's squat figure. Forming an immediate fondness for Roselina, Maddie returned Linc's affectionate smile.

Releasing Maddie and patting her long, golden hair, Roselina said, "And I was expecting a little girl, not a grown-up woman. Why'd you fib to me, Mr. Linc?"

"I was surprised, too, Roselina. I was expecting the little girl I'd remembered."

"Well, you're pretty as a picture, Miss Maddie. Let me show you to your room, and then we'll have a little snack before you take a rest. I know what a tiresome trip it is from the mainland. My two kids live in California, and I go to see them once a year. It takes a day or two to rest from the long flight."

Recalling Ahonui's comment about Maddie's reputation, Linc cleared his throat. "I've been thinking,

Roselina, that Maddie might be more comfortable in the guesthouse. It's ready for company, isn't it?"

Roselina's startled eyes met her employer's, then she took another, appraising look at Maddie. "Of course, Mr. Linc," Roselina said quickly. "She will have more privacy. Come this way, Miss Maddie."

As Maddie followed Roselina to the small cottage, she wondered at this sudden change in where she was staying. Maybe she hadn't lived up to Linc's expectations, and he didn't want her around all the time. Maddie knew she should curb her sensitive nature, but it was hard to break a lifelong habit. She'd always found it difficult to believe that people really wanted her for a friend.

"You'll like the cottage better than the bedroom in the house," Roselina said as she walked next to Maddie. When the housekeeper opened the door to the one-room cottage, Maddie agreed with her.

"Oh, this is wonderful," she said. The bedroom and bathroom area were separated from the combination kitchen and living room by a wooden screen. "Listen to the ocean waves. What a peaceful place to sleep. But why do you need a cottage when the house is so large?"

"Long ago, this was the office of the plantation owner, and Mr. Linc thought it would make a good guesthouse. He entertains business friends here sometimes, so I keep it ready for use." She opened the small refrigerator. "Soft drinks and ice are in here." Pointing to a box on the wall, she said. "Intercom to the house. Also a private phone if you want to call home. Nice, huh?"

"Very nice." The room was warm so Maddie laid her jacket and purse on the small couch. By the time Roselina had shown her where the extra towels and blankets were kept, Linc arrived with her luggage.

"Do I have time to take a shower and change before lunch?"

"Yes, take your time. I've prepared cold snacks for lunch, and I can serve them when you're ready," Roselina assured her.

Trotting beside Linc as they returned to the main house, Roselina demanded, "Why isolate the little thing when there's a nice room all ready in the house?"

Flushing slightly, Linc said, "Yes, a nice room directly across the hall from mine. I really didn't expect Maddie to be so…" He hesitated. "So mature. She'll prefer the privacy of the guesthouse."

Ahonui's remarks had made Linc more conscious of his responsibility while Maddie visited him. And he hadn't been prepared for the emotional jolt Maddie's appearance had caused. Since Stanley Horton had been his friend, Maddie probably thought of him as a father figure, and he'd have to be sure that he kept it that way. Trouble was, he didn't know how a father should act, either. But he knew that he would be more comfortable if Maddie didn't occupy the bedroom across the hall from his own.

When Maddie showed up for lunch wearing white

capris, a coral tunic and a pair of white canvas sandals, Linc groaned inwardly. The casual garments she'd exchanged for the light blue tailored suit she'd worn made her even more attractive. How could he spend a month treating Maddie as the daughter of his friend when he suspected that she embodied the traits he'd looked for in a woman most of his adult life? Since he didn't date much, his friends often accused him of being too picky. And maybe he was, because he hadn't found anyone before whose presence affected him as Maddie's did.

After lunch, Maddie said, "I'm very tired, but I'd like to take a walk down to the beach before I go to bed. I'm too keyed up to sleep yet."

"Just take a little nap," Roselina advised, "and tonight you can get adjusted to the local sleeping schedule."

"I'll show you around," Linc said.

Narrow stepping stones marked the path to the beach, and they walked single file. Following Maddie, Linc carried two lounge chairs.

"It's a small beach but fairly private except for pleasure boats traveling by." Gesturing in a wide arc toward the palatial hotels dominating the coastline in both directions, he said, "You can see we're situated in a cove between several large resort hotels."

Maddie kicked off her sandals, walked across the sandy beach and waded into the gentle surf. "I can't believe it," she said, jumping up and down, splashing water in her excitement. "Maddie Horton walking in the Pacific Ocean. I must be dreaming. Is it safe to swim here?"

"Perfectly safe," Linc assured her. "I usually take a swim when I come home from work."

"My swimsuit is in the piece of luggage we'll pick up tomorrow, so I can't swim today."

Linc unfolded the lounge chairs. "We can sit and enjoy the view until you get sleepy."

Maddie stretched out on the chair, leaned her head back and listened to the regular rhythm of the incoming whitecaps. A large white bird with red feet landed on the beach and strutted serenely through the water, turning its head toward Linc and Maddie as if expecting a handout.

"Is that a seagull?"

"We don't have seagulls in Hawaii. That's a Red-footed Booby."

Maddie frowned. "What an ugly name for such a pretty bird."

"You'll notice many birds that are strange to you. There's a bird book in your cottage for guests—you can use that to identify them."

The long plane trip had been exhausting and Maddie sighed. Despite the disturbing news she'd read about the naval officer's death, she had never felt more content in her life. These few hours with Linc had proven he was the same thoughtful, caring man who'd supported Maddie and her mother through Stanley Horton's funeral years ago. She went to sleep wondering if Linc was in love with Ahonui.

Linc unashamedly watched Maddie as she slept. The breeze whiffed the long golden tresses around her face, and occasionally Maddie brushed them aside. Her face was relaxed and she seemed vulnerable, as if she was still the girl he remembered, but she wasn't a child. Nor did he want her to be, although he didn't dare hope that she would regard him romantically. Maddie sighed wearily and an agonized expression spread across her face.

Suddenly Linc felt like a Peeping Tom, and he turned on his side away from Maddie, but not to sleep. The recent news that an investigation was being initiated into Stanley Horton's death had come as a shock to him. If he'd had any notion of such a development, he wouldn't have invited Maddie to visit. He didn't want to ruin her vacation, but she should be made aware of these new developments. What was the best way to tell her? He decided to say nothing until she had rested.

They ate their evening meal of chicken, potatoes and mixed vegetables in the dining room with a full view of the Pacific.

"Except for some of the spices, this meal could have been served back home," Maddie said. "I'm curious about what kind of food you prepare for Christmas. And how do you celebrate here in Hawaii? Are your customs different?"

Laughing, Linc said, "Different from what I knew as a kid. I grew up in Iowa, and I remember going to

Grandma's house for a traditional Christmas dinner. We didn't travel in a horse-drawn sleigh, but we had snow most of the time. You obviously won't see any snow, but people do a lot of decorating. And we serve ham and turkey with all the fixin's in my restaurants and people like that. I heard a news anchor say last week that you can always tell you're spending Christmas in Hawaii when 'Silent Night' is played on a ukulele and Santa arrives on the beach in a canoe."

"That's funny," she said with a grin. "I've been thinking how strange it will seem to spend Christmas Day at the beach. Do you decorate a tree?"

As Roselina cleared the table for dessert, she said, "Christmas trees are brought in by ship—sometimes by plane. Mr. Linc usually brings home a fir tree, and I decorate it for him. European seamen brought Christmas to the islands, but I don't think much attention was paid to the holiday until Hawaii became a U.S. territory."

"I read in the newspaper last week that the first Christmas was supposedly celebrated in Hawaii when an English ship captain and his crew observed the holiday in the South Pacific not far from here." Linc grinned and added, "Their menu consisted of roasted pig and coconut milk. I've always served roasted pork at my restaurants, and this year, as a specialty for the Christmas season, we're serving chilled coconut milk."

Mention of the newspaper reminded Maddie of

the article. Suddenly the joy of celebrating Christmas in Hawaii took second place to the suspicion that her father could have been murdered.

Noting her change of expression, as soon as they finished the meal, Linc asked Maddie if she wanted to go to her cottage.

Stifling a yawn, she said, "But I should help Roselina with the dishes."

"No, no," the housekeeper said. "I have a dishwasher, and it will take no time. You can help next time, but you should rest your first night here."

As soon as the sun set, darkness came immediately, and Maddie felt apprehensive. She willingly agreed when Linc said, "I'll walk with you to the cottage. I don't have dusk to dawn lights because I like the peace of total darkness, but it might be intimidating if you aren't used to it."

He turned on the light over the garage door, which was near the cottage. "I'll leave this light on all night."

Maddie thanked him, because the darkness did frighten her. And it was deathly quiet except for the continuous slapping of waves on the beach.

"Sleep as late as you want," Linc said, "and when you're ready, come to the house for breakfast. We'll spend the next two days in Honolulu visiting the World War II sites that you want to see and also laze around on Waikiki Beach for a few hours."

He opened the door. Hesitantly, she said, "Do you have time to come in?"

Wondering, he said, "Yes, of course."

"I want to show you something."

Maddie went into the bedroom area and returned with the newspaper she'd gotten on the plane. She spread it out before him and pointed to the article that had disturbed her. "Do you know anything about this?"

Linc threaded his fingers through his thick hair. "I'm sorry you found out before I had a chance to tell you. If you've read the paper, you know as much as I do. The prison break was reported on television, but since residents have both English and Hawaiian names, at first I didn't connect the escapees with your father's death. Since the military is doing the investigation, they won't release much information, but I'm sure that it is Commander Horton's death."

"Will you tell me about Daddy's death? I'm sure I heard details of the accident when I was a child, but Mother didn't like to talk about it. I don't remember what really happened."

"Yes, I will, but shouldn't we wait until tomorrow? You must be tired, and if we start talking about this tonight, you probably won't go to sleep."

"You're right, of course."

His eyes were compassionate as he said, "It must have been a jolt for you to learn about this new development when you're so far from your family and friends."

"Actually, I don't really have a family. I'm an only child, and except for a few cousins I rarely see, there isn't anyone. My grandmother died soon after my mother did. After that, you know that I spent two years at the Valley of Hope."

Linc nodded, and she continued, "And the last two years I've lived in a college dorm. I've gone to school winter and summer because I didn't have anything else to do. I have some very special friends, however, and I'm thankful for them."

"I guess we have a lot in common. I'm an only child, too, and I joined the navy after my parents died in a car accident. I have several aunts and uncles and lots of cousins, but we don't keep in touch. My fault, not theirs."

Stifling another yawn, Maddie said, "Because I don't have any home ties, I do appreciate this invitation to visit you. Christmas has always been a sad time for me, so I'm determined to enjoy myself while I'm here despite this disturbing news, which may concern Daddy."

Linc squeezed her hand gently.

"Hey, I'm a loner, too," he said with a gentle smile. "The pleasure is mine. You're going to keep me from being lonely this Christmas." Tugging gently on her hair, he laughed and said, "Once you get used to the angels in the nativity scenes wearing leis instead of halos, you'll enjoy Christmas in Hawaii."

Maddie stood in the door and watched Linc's long stride as he returned to the house. His last words sounded as if he was speaking to a child. Why did that annoy her?

THREE

After the long flight, Maddie had expected to fall asleep quickly. The bed was comfortable, the room was cool, and she was irritated when she flounced until the covers resembled a war zone. She couldn't stop thinking about Linc. The affection she'd harbored for him since she'd first met him had been like a child's security blanket. Following the death of her father, she'd needed a physical reminder to keep his memory alive in her heart and mind. Linc had been that reminder.

During her teen years, after her mother had gotten ill, she'd also needed an anchor, and Linc's memory had provided that. Thinking of Linc as her special friend had helped her bear the loss of both parents. Although their contact had been infrequent, she'd remembered him in her heart as a sort of knight in shining armor. She had imagined him to be all that was good, noble and caring. How did the Linc she'd met today measure up to her dream man?

Maddie groaned, turned on her stomach and buried

her head in the pillow. Linc was even more charming than she had ever imagined. Would spending a month with him bring her a lot of grief? He obviously thought of her as a child. And what about his relationship with Ahonui? If she allowed herself to fall in love with Linc, would she go home with a broken heart?

Tears stained the pillow before Maddie finally fell sleep, but she awakened at daylight. She showered and dressed for the day in jeans and a blue-and-white stripped tunic-length cotton shirt. Since her fair skin burned easily, she thought the cuffed three-quarter-length sleeves would be helpful. The shirttail hem allowed the blouse to hang loosely about her hips. She put on the sandals she'd worn yesterday. She hadn't brought many clothes, because she hoped to buy a few locally made garments.

Linc hadn't said what time Roselina served breakfast, but since it wasn't yet seven o'clock, she walked to the beach. The tide was out, and she picked up several small shells to take to her friend Lucy. She stepped out of her shoes to test the temperature of the water. It was cool, but not too cold, and she thought she could easily swim each morning.

Hearing a sound behind her, Maddie turned and waved to Linc, who walked toward her. He wore white walking shorts and a red knit shirt. Her heart fluttered like a leaf caught in a strong wind, and this reaction to Linc's appearance irritated her. What had happened to her common sense?

"You're up early," he said.

"I couldn't sleep. My mind and body are still operating on Eastern Standard Time."

"That happens sometimes," he said. "It will take a day or two for you to get over jet lag."

Laughing up at him, Maddie said, "I didn't realize what jet lag was until I woke up before dawn this morning."

"Ready for breakfast?" Linc said. "Roselina has everything prepared. I have a full day planned for you."

"Such as?"

"Since you want to research World War II in Hawaii, I'll take you to the Punch Bowl Cemetery to see the memorial to the men who died in that war. We'll also go to Pearl Harbor and visit the USS *Arizona* memorial. After you get a general view of these historic places, you can do more detailed research if you like."

"I'm planning to collect books and pamphlets, as well as take pictures. I brought some disposable cameras with me."

Roselina served breakfast on the patio. In the distance, large ships plied the open waters of the Pacific. Palm trees along the coast swayed like ballerinas in the mild breeze. Sun had warmed the air, but the breeze had a cooling effect.

Sipping on a glass of pineapple juice, Maddie said, "This can't be me—Maddie Horton—in paradise. We'd already had snow and some zero temperatures before I left home. Pinch me so I can tell if I'm dreaming."

Playfully, Linc reached across the table and pinched her arm lightly. It was a simple gesture, but an electrifying one. Blue eyes looked into gray ones, and for a moment the universe seemed to stand still, as if they were seeing each other for the first time.

Coming out on the patio with a tray, Roselina said, "Here's a—" She stopped abruptly. But her words had broken the spell. Linc shook his head and felt his face reddening as he expelled the breath he'd been holding. Maddie clutched a napkin in her hands and looked away.

Groaning inwardly, Linc wondered how to deal with the unbidden emotion that had suddenly filled his heart. If he thought the attraction was one-sided, it would be easier, but he was convinced that Maddie had experienced a similar reaction. He would have to keep reminding her and himself of the eleven years difference in their ages.

He turned to Roselina who stared at him—speechless for a change. Clearing his throat, he said, "Are you going to keep us in suspense? Have you made one of your special omelets?"

"Of course, Mr. Linc! Special food for a special guest."

She took the lid off the serving dish and swept the tempting omelet onto the table between them. "You like omelets, Miss Maddie?"

"I've bought them in restaurants lots of times. I've never eaten a homemade one."

"Then you're in for a treat," Linc said. The difficult moment passed, but it wasn't forgotten by any of them.

After they finished the meal, Linc pushed back from the table and propped his right ankle on the opposite knee. Roselina poured another cup of coffee for him and brought hot tea for Maddie. Preparing a cup of tea for herself, she joined them at the table.

"This is as good a time as any to tell you what I know about your father's death," Linc said. "He was sent to Hawaii on a short-term assignment to test a new plane the navy wanted to purchase. While he was here, he investigated and brought about the arrest of some Hawaiian employees who were stealing military supplies and technology and selling them to foreign governments."

Shocked at this disclosure, Maddie gasped, "I've never heard that. I'm sure Mother didn't tell me."

"She probably didn't want to worry you," Roselina said "Mothers are like that."

With a somber face, Linc continued, "A father and two sons were involved in the theft. The father was killed resisting arrest at the time. The sons were imprisoned, but they escaped from prison a few days ago. The oldest son was recaptured and died from wounds he'd received while trying to escape. Before he died he confessed that he'd been involved in the death of Commander Horton. He's a member of an ancient Polynesian cult that practice 'a life for a life' religion. To his way of thinking, Stanley Horton had caused his father's death, so he sabotaged the plane Stanley was flying."

"That's sounds medieval," Maddie said, shocked. "I didn't know anything like that went on anymore."

"Not many people in the islands hold to the old ways, but there are a few. The police think the other escapee was injured, but he hasn't been captured yet." Getting up from the table, he reached his right hand to Maddie. "Don't think about it. Let's get started so you can see Honolulu."

But he wasn't sure he wanted Honolulu to see her. Well rested, she was even lovelier than she'd been when she'd arrived yesterday.

Since they had two hours before they could enter the Pearl Harbor memorial, he drove to the Punch Bowl Cemetery. Maddie took several photos of the whole area and close-up shots of the towering memorial to World War II veterans.

A motor launch quickly took them from the mainland to the site of the USS *Arizona*. Maddie's lips trembled and tears misted her eyes as she looked at the pieces of the ship still visible through the waters after more than fifty years. She scanned the long list of those entombed in the wreckage during the air raid that had plunged the United States into World War II. The deaths of these servicemen made more vivid poignant memories of her own father's death.

Linc had been aware of the sadness Maddie was experiencing. When they returned to the launch to take them back to the main island, tears slowly slid down her cheeks. He wiped them away with his handkerchief, and throwing caution to the wind, he put his arm around her. She leaned her head on his shoulder. When they reached the dock, she looked up at him with grateful eyes. "Thanks," she said, and he squeezed her hand as he helped her out of the boat.

"I'm not sure I can write a paper on this subject," she said. "It's such a sad chapter in the history of our country, I don't know if I can deal with it."

"Don't make up your mind now. Every war has had its tragedies. Too bad nations can't learn to live in peace."

He left the parking lot and turned toward the city of Honolulu, thinking it was time for Maddie's mind to be diverted from the horrors of war. She'd had enough tragedy in her young life. Had he made a mistake to take her to the war memorials before she saw the lighter side of Hawaii?

Maddie had heard of Waikiki Beach all of her life, and when she knew she'd be coming to visit Linc, she'd rented a travel video about the beaches of Hawaii. But the film hadn't prepared her for the beauty of this area—the tall, swaying palm trees, the wide sandy beach, the sun shimmering on the tranquil water.

They accessed the beach on the western end, and the first thing to catch her eye was Diamond Head a few miles down the coast. Then she looked seaward at the blue, placid Pacific where people were swimming, surfboarding or riding in outrigger canoes. Others lay on the beach under tents, and numerous visitors sunbathed in lounge chairs.

"Oh, I love it! I love it!" Maddie said. "Makes me wish I lived near an ocean. I can see I've missed a lot of fun things."

It seemed natural for them to hold hands as they strolled along the walkway.

"I'll see that you experience Hawaii to the fullest before you go home."

So intent was Maddie on looking at everything, she didn't notice the frequent stares of the men along the walkway. But Linc noticed, and he didn't appreciate their attention.

When they approached a man holding two gaily plumaged birds, Linc asked, "Do you want to have your picture taken with one of the birds?"

Maddie nodded and her eyes gleamed with excitement when the man placed one of the birds on her shoulder.

"How about you, sir?" he said. "Get in the picture." Linc held out his arm and the other bird perched on it. "Stand close to the young lady."

The man snapped two pictures on his instant camera, and when they developed he handed them to Maddie for viewing.

"Do you like them?" Linc asked.

Maddie didn't like the tense expression in her eyes—just as the man had snapped the picture, the bird had squeezed her ear with his beak. Surprise shone from her eyes, and her body was tense—as if she was ready to jump out of her skin. But Linc's picture was perfect. "Yes," she said. "They will make good souvenirs." She would have that picture to add to the other one she'd had for years.

Linc handed the man a ten-dollar bill, and Maddie held the still-moist pictures carefully as they went on their way.

They bought colas and hot dogs and ate in a picnic shelter that faced the water. Maddie purchased postcards to send to Miss Caroline and her friends, Lucy Harrison and Janice Reid. Linc rented two beach chairs under an umbrella made of dried palm leaves, and while she wrote to her friends, he dozed in the shade. She'd never felt more at peace with the world.

"Tell me about your restaurants," Maddie said when she finished her cards and put them in her tote bag.

"I have one on each of the four major islands," he said. "Eight years ago, I started with a small restaurant here in Honolulu and expanded it over the next two years. When that business was paid for, I started a restaurant on Maui, which also became successful. Over the next two years I opened restaurants on Hawaii and Kauai. It's been a slow process, but I didn't have much money to start with."

"Are you through expanding?"

"I'm in the process of opening another restaurant here in Honolulu."

"What kind of restaurants?"

"They're called Everyday Luau. Luaus are big tourist attractions in Hawaii, but expensive. My restaurants have all of the qualities of a luau, but on a smaller scale, and at much less cost."

"I don't understand."

"We serve the same foods available at a luau. There's a nightly entertainment of traditional Hawaiian music. Each restaurant has a gift shop stocking Hawaiian gift items usually found at luaus. You'll see what I mean tonight. We're eating dinner at the Everyday Luau a few blocks from here."

Maddie looked down at her casual clothes. "Dressed like this?"

"Sure. We've created an outdoor atmosphere inside the restaurants. There will be more guests in shorts and jeans than dresses and sport coats."

"It sounds like fun."

"I think so," Linc said.

But Linc's explanation hadn't prepared Maddie for the romantic atmosphere of Everyday Luau. The exterior of the metal building located several blocks from downtown Honolulu wasn't impressive. As she stepped inside, however, Maddie felt as if she'd entered a beach resort. She stopped, awe-struck, inside the front door and looked with wondering eyes.

Wall hangings of the ocean and beach, as well as several live palm trees, presented an outdoor atmosphere. The sound of a teeming ocean filtered through the speaker system. Chinese lanterns hung from the ceiling giving out a dim light. The waitresses were dressed in identical gaily flowered muumuus. The waiters' shirts matched the dresses.

When she commented on the garments, Linc

said, "They have different costumes for each night of the week."

Linc always enjoyed bringing guests to experience the uniqueness of his restaurants, but he'd never been more interested in anyone's reaction than he was in Maddie's.

"We'll have to take our seats," he said, and she followed the waitress to a table for two beneath a palm tree on a raised platform. Their chairs faced the stage and commanded a sweeping view of the restaurant.

Buffet centers were located throughout the room.

The waitress brought water and took their orders for other beverages. Traditional music filtered quietly around them. The lights faded into semidarkness, and a hush fell over the restaurant. Suddenly two torchbearers ran through the room lighting the tall piers that blazed brightly, illuminating the interior.

"Actually, this is a symbolic ritual," Linc whispered. "We can't have open flames inside the building. The torches themselves are electric."

"But it's so beautiful. And you have four of these restaurants!"

"Yes, but this one is the largest."

Kalua pork, the featured meat of early luaus, graced the buffet tables, along with chicken and long rice, salmon, all kinds of vegetables, salads and desserts. Several of the items Maddie took on her plate were unusual. She didn't always know what she was eating, but the food was delicious. She especially liked coconut bread. She sipped slowly a glass of chilled coconut milk that Linc had added for the Christmas season as a special tribute to the Europeans who had first observed Christmas in the islands.

"I could soon get used to this kind of living," she said to Linc when she took the last bite of rhubarb angel food cake. "Thanks again for inviting me to visit you. I'm learning a whole new way of life. We lived on the naval base in San Diego when I was a child. That's the farthest I've been away from my birthplace."

"Your father was stationed at San Diego when I enlisted, and I was really pleased when he was trans-ferred to Hawaii. If he had stayed here, he intended to bring you and your mother."

"Unfortunately, Mother wasn't a good service-man's wife. She didn't like the restrictions of a naval base, and I doubt if she would have left her parents to move to Hawaii."

Suddenly, Maddie felt uneasy. She looked around and saw a husky Hawaiian staring at her with bold, malicious eyes. He dodged behind a palm tree and chills chased up Maddie's spine. She wanted to think he'd been staring at someone else, but she knew there wasn't another table behind them.

Linc noted Maddie's change of expression, and he figured she was saddened by thoughts of her father's death. He welcomed the flickering lights indicating the start of the evening's entertainment.

The current program illustrated the crafts and

culture of several islands making up the Polynesian group. Interspersed with the music was a demonstration of the making of tapa cloth from mulberry bark. Tonga Fire came alive as a Samoan rubbed sticks together. Natives from New Zealand acted out one of their ancestral legends. Hawaiian girls demonstrated the hula dance.

The hour-long show closed when one man and two women accompanied themselves on a guitar and two ukuleles to sing a medley of hymns. Their closing number, "God Be With You Till We Meet Again" brought tears to Maddie's eyes.

The restaurant presented a different entertainment each night of the week, but Linc was familiar with them, and he watched Maddie rather than the show. He didn't have to ask if she liked the program. Her expression changed from interest, to delight, to awe, to pleasure. She had seen so little of the world. What would it be like to guide her as she visited other cultures?

Clutching a cloth to his bleeding side, Kamu struggled up the steep incline and fell face forward on the stone step of the secluded cabin that had been his refuge for the past two weeks. His race was run, and his heart was heavy because he had failed to avenge the deaths of the other male members of his family. He faced eternity without hope because he hadn't kept faith with his ancestors.

An hour later, Edena stumbled over the body of

her twin brother as she started into the cabin. As hefty as her brother, Edena had no trouble lifting him. She carried the last remaining male member of her family carefully into the cabin and laid him on the narrow cot. When she peeled back Kamu's shirt, blood spurted from the wound he'd received when he escaped from prison. She heated some water and although her hands probed gently when she removed the blood-soaked bandage, Kamu groaned and his eyes opened.

"Sister," he whispered, and his eyes brightened. "I will not have to die alone."

"You shall not die," she said. "Aumakua will not permit it."

Kamu shook his head wearily. "Our god, Aumakua, does not listen to me now. I'm the only one left, and I have failed to honor my forebears. Give me a knife. If I die by my own hand, it will suffice."

Edena stretched herself to her full five-feet-five-inches height, pounded herself on the chest and said haughtily, "You forget me. I am willing to carry on the family honor."

"But you're a woman. That will shame me."

"Then I will become a man—at least part of the time. Rest in peace, Kamu."

Throughout the remainder of the night, Edena sat beside her brother, holding his hand as he slowly and painfully died. Her thoughts were not so much on her brother as on Stanley Horton, who had brought tragedy to her family. It had started when Horton had discovered their crime. One by one, she'd seen her family taken from her. Someone must pay.

When her brother died at last, Edena wept and mourned audibly for hours. As the day dawned, she stood before a small cracked mirror and with a small hammer, knocked out one of her front teeth—a custom of bereavement in her family.

With blood spilling from her mouth, she shouldered her brother's body and walked up a rugged mountain to the secret family burial cave. She attached a rope to the joints of his legs, put the rope behind his neck and tightened the rope until his knees touched his chest. She wrapped the flexed body in a coarse cloth and placed the rounded package on a shelf in the cave. She laid her hand on the body of her twin and muttered, alternating from her native language to English, *"He ola na he ola*—a life for a life."

She passed by the interment alcoves of the other members of the family. When she touched each bundle, she muttered, "A life for a life—I will avenge."

Edena carefully parted the brushy covering before she stepped out of the cave. A bitter smile twisted her lips as she plodded down the mountain, never doubting that she would be victorious in her vengeance.

FOUR

Whether it was the strenuous, fun-filled day she'd enjoyed on Saturday, or whether her body was adjusting to the time change, Maddie woke on Sunday morning feeling rested and at peace with the world. Roselina had said that she always slept in on Sunday morning, so Maddie checked the clock and knew that she had time for a dip in the Pacific.

She put on the white, skirted tank suit she'd bought on sale in September, never realizing then that she'd be in Hawaii when she wore it. She wrapped herself in a terry robe and slipped her feet into a pair of leather scuffs. She put her Bible in her tote bag, intending to have her morning devotions on the beach. Taking a large towel from the bathroom, she walked toward the water.

The sun filtered through the slight haze hovering over the water. A gray bird with white feathers below its wings flew along the shoreline. Linc had identified several of the native birds when they walked along Waikiki yesterday. Maddie recognized this one as a sooty tern.

The ocean breeze was cool, but invigorating. She spread the towel beside the water, took off her shoes and sat on the towel close enough to the ocean to invite an occasional wave to splash over her feet. She opened her Bible to the book of Psalms. When Maddie worshipped outdoors, her thoughts always turned to the writings of David. It seemed strange to her that although he'd lived in an arid environment, the psalmist had an acute comprehension of the ocean.

Reading aloud, she used the words of David from Psalm 104 for her morning prayer.

"'O Lord, how manifold are Thy works! In wisdom hast thou made them all: the earth is full of Thy riches. So is this great and wide sea, wherein are things creeping innumerable, both small and great beasts. There go the ships; there is that leviathan, whom Thou hast made to play therein. These wait upon Thee.'"

When Linc had taken her on the submarine tour off Waikiki Beach yesterday, she'd marveled at the vast number of fish populating the ocean. How had the psalmist known that?

Taking off her robe, Maddie walked carefully into the waves, but the water was cooler than she'd thought, and she didn't tarry long. She'd been too sleepy last night when they'd gotten home to ask Linc about a church, but she was eager to attend worship services. She returned to the cottage, showered and dressed for the day in a pastel blue skirt set. The calf-length print skirt had dark blue and white flowers, and the short-sleeved cotton sweater hung below her waist. The outfit appeared to add height to her body. She had been extremely conscious of her petite figure when she'd walked beside Linc and Ahonui.

Linc had been sitting on the glass-enclosed balcony on the second floor when Maddie walked to the beach. For a moment he was tempted to join her, but considering the emotions she'd stirred in his heart, he knew it was wise for them to do their swimming separately. He got up from his chair immediately, because he didn't want Maddie to see him and think he was spying on her. However, if she should encounter any danger, he needed to know, so he walked to the shadow of the hallway to stand guard. When she returned to her cottage, he got ready for the day.

After they finished breakfast, Linc said, "Tomorrow, we'll start island hopping, but today is a good time to take a driving tour of Oahu. You'll want to see more of our country than the tourist things we'll be visiting the next three days."

"I thought we'd go to church this morning," she said, looking down at her garments.

"Oh, I hadn't thought about that," Linc said. "I haven't gone to church in years."

"More shame to you," Roselina said as she took away the breakfast dishes.

Maddie turned startled blue eyes on Linc. Her

heart plummeted. She'd finally found a chink in Linc's armor. Her faith in God was an integral part of her life. It saddened her to find out that Linc didn't share her Christian beliefs.

"You can go to church with me, Miss Maddie," Roselina said. "I leave at half-past nine."

"Oh, I'll take you, Maddie," Linc said quickly. "I'm a member of the church Roselina goes to. I support the work financially, but I seldom attend the services."

Roselina's appraising eyes swept his face, and Linc wouldn't meet her eyes. No matter what his housekeeper thought, it was his responsibility to look after Maddie.

Although she wanted Linc to go with her, Maddie said, "I'd like to have you go to church with me, but not if you don't want to. I'll go with Roselina."

Standing to pull back her chair, Linc said, "I *want* to take you. I'll go change. Roselina, you might as well ride with us."

"No, thank you. I'm visiting my sister this afternoon. I'll go to her home from the church."

The church, located in a small seaside village, was a frame building with a white steeple. Linc pointed out some damage to the structure from the previous year's hurricane. The sign over the door indicated that the congregation had been organized in the late nineteenth century.

The sanctuary wouldn't have seated more than seventy-five people, and it was barely half-full. The pastor was a native of Tennessee who'd come to Hawaii for his health. The service he conducted was similar to the kind that Maddie had known all of her life.

The people were friendly, and she felt right at home, but Linc fidgeted, as if he were uncomfortable. Was his conscience hurting him because he hadn't been coming to church? Or was he sorry he'd volunteered to come with her?

Linc had been impressed with the pastor when he'd met him previously, and he thought his sermon on the parable of the prodigal son was well planned. He presented it effectively. But the text cut straight to Linc's heart. Had God planned this message especially for him? To close his message, the minister emphasized his text once again:

Father, I have sinned against heaven and against you. I am no longer worthy to be called your son… So he got up and went to his father.

Linc took stock of his spiritual self, realizing how far he'd strayed from his Father's house. He slanted a sideways glance at Maddie, whose face mirrored contentment and peace as she focused her attention on the message. Had it taken Maddie's example of innocent faith to call attention to his lack of devotion to God?

Maddie was more talkative than usual as they drove home. Linc concluded that her strength of character and her deep faith had developed through a consistent fellowship with other Christians. This gave him much to think about when considering his relationship with Maddie. In addition to the age difference between them, Linc knew he lacked the faith Maddie would expect in any man she dated.

Linc unlocked the door of the house, saying, "Roselina has Sunday afternoon and evenings off. I usually just snack during that time—I'm not a cook. We can go out for lunch, or we can have a sandwich and eat our evening meal before we come back from our drive. What would you rather do?"

"Let's eat here. I'll help you, although I haven't done much cooking since I went to VOH four years ago. Except for breakfast, I eat most of my meals in the university cafeteria. Lucy and I have a refrigerator and microwave in our room, and we heat rolls, bagels and stuff like that for breakfast."

Heading toward the kitchen, Linc said, "Roselina wanted to fix our lunch, but I put my foot down. She needs time to herself. I told her we could manage."

"You're fortunate to have her."

"I'll say," he agreed as he rummaged in the fridge. He set out cold cuts, condiments and a variety of bread.

"How about some melon, too?" he said. "Roselina has a bowl prepared. She doesn't pay much attention to my orders," he admitted with a slight laugh. "Sometimes, I wonder who the boss is around here."

Maddie smiled with him. She'd already decided that Roselina had a mind of her own.

"I like melon. We can eat that for dessert."

He shook his head. "She's made a coconut cream pie, but I'll leave it in the refrigerator until we're ready for dessert. We'll eat the melon with our sandwiches. If you make them, I'll take plates and cups to the patio. What do you want to drink?"

"Just water with lemon."

"All right. Two glasses of iced water coming up." He filled the glasses with ice, dropped in a chunk of lemon that Roselina had also provided and turned to the sink. Maddie spread four slices of brown bread with mayonnaise and added cheese and ham. She heard the front door open, and her hands stilled when Ahonui Kingsbury walked into the kitchen.

"Good, we're just in time for lunch," she said, and her eyes seemed to challenge Linc. A man entered the kitchen behind Ahonui, and thinking that it might be Ahonui's husband or boyfriend, Maddie was pleased. Her pleasure ended when Ahonui said, "I wanted my brother, Steve, to meet you, Maddie."

Linc filled the two glasses before he turned to greet the Kingsburys. Why was Ahonui taking such an interest in Maddie? He and Roselina entertained the Kingsburys occasionally, but Ahonui had never just dropped in like this before. Today's visit irritated him, and since he wasn't always able to keep his emotions from showing on his face, there was a tense moment in the kitchen.

Linc resented the appraising way Steve looked at

Maddie, but he forced himself to say amiably, "Hello, Steve."

Ahonui put her purse on one of the kitchen chairs. "I'll make our sandwiches," she said. She took the bread and lunch meat from Maddie's hands and started fashioning more sandwiches.

Controlling his temper, Linc said, "You're welcome to have lunch with us, but Maddie and I are leaving in an hour."

"Any place we can tag along?" Ahonui asked.

"No," Linc answered and reached into the cabinet for two more place settings. "Steve, we're eating on the patio. Why don't you carry these out?"

Maddie could sense tension during the meal. She tried to determine the relationship between Linc and Ahonui. She had thought Linc was irritated when the Kingsburys showed up, but he was civil to them, so perhaps she had imagined that. Once again she wondered if he was romantically involved with her.

Much of the conversation around the table was between Linc and Ahonui concerning business matters that had come up during the two days he'd been away from the office. But after they'd finished their sandwiches, Steve turned to Maddie.

"Are you enjoying your visit?" he asked.

"Very much. It seems like a wonderful place to live."

"It has its drawbacks," he said. "Most people who come here from mainland U.S.A. like it at first, but they soon get tired of it. It's very confining, you know. People who are used to driving hundreds of miles in any direction don't stay here very long. I'm thinking about moving—perhaps to Japan."

Steve was a chunky, swarthy man. His face was darker than Ahonui's, and he didn't have his sister's handsome features. He had a habit of looking over Maddie's left shoulder as he talked to her, a mannerism she found disconcerting. She kept wanting to look behind her. She noticed that although Linc seemed intent on what Ahonui was saying, he often glanced toward her and Steve, as if he was monitoring their conversation.

"Do you work in Honolulu, Mr. Kingsbury?"

"Yes, and please, call me Steve. I have a boat rental on Waikiki."

"Linc and I were there yesterday. Did you see us?"

"No. I played golf yesterday."

They tarried over their luncheon until Linc looked at his watch. "Maddie, we should get started. If you want to go to the cottage and change, I'll clear away the dishes. We'll leave in thirty minutes."

"It won't take that long for me to get out of this dress and into something more casual," she said. "I'll help put the things in the dishwasher. You and Roselina are spoiling me."

Picking up her own plate and silverware, Ahonui cast a speculative glance at Maddie. "So you're staying in the guesthouse."

"Yes, and it's a perfect place. I love hearing the ocean waves when I wake up in the morning."

"When are you coming back to work, Linc?" Ahonui asked.

"I have appointments on Friday, so I'll be back by then. Maybe Thursday. We're going to Kauai tomorrow and on to Hawaii before we come home. I don't have a set itinerary."

"You mean to skip Maui?" Steve said.

"We'll go there after Christmas," Linc said.

"Well, I can contact you on your cell phone if I need you," Ahonui said.

"If you do, leave a message. I'll keep it turned off and check mail once a day. Too many people have my phone number, and I don't want to be bothered all the time we're traveling."

Maddie hurried to the guesthouse and changed into a pair of shorts and a knit shirt, unable to comprehend that it could be snowing at home. She picked up her camera and locked the door behind her. Linc waited for her by the garage. The Kingsburys were already in their car.

"Sorry to keep you waiting," she said.

"You didn't—we just came from the house."

Ahonui and Steve followed them out of the driveway, and Linc said, "I'll be surprised if they don't follow us."

"I don't want to cause any trouble. If there's work you need to do, don't bother with me. I can entertain myself."

Turning left on the highway, Linc looked in the rearview to see which way Steve headed. To his surprise, and relief, the Kingsburys turned to the right.

"Ahonui knew I planned to take at least a week to show you around the islands. Sometimes she takes her work position too seriously. I do appreciate her loyalty, but I *am* the boss and I don't let her dictate my personal life. Relax and enjoy yourself."

Linc drove across the mountains to the northern side of Oahu. He was amused and pleased at Maddie's childlike enjoyment of the scenery. She exclaimed over the spectacular rugged views on their left, as well as the broad, flat areas that led down to the Pacific.

"We're going to the Polynesian Cultural Center," Linc explained. "The center is probably the favorite tourist attraction in the islands. I'll explain a bit about it as we drive. I see you brought your camera, so let me know if you want to stop and take pictures. You'll see some pretty sights."

"I did a little research before I left home, so I know that Hawaii is part of a large group of islands collectively known as the Polynesian Islands."

He glanced at her approvingly. "That's true. The center is a nonprofit organization to preserve Polynesian cultural heritage. Most of the people you'll see today are students at a nearby university. Fees at the center provide scholarships for many of the students."

They were greeted at the gateway to the center by

two women, who put shell leis around their necks. Judging by their clothing, Linc told Maddie that they were from Tahiti. Although there were many exhibits to view, Linc chose only three, the ones he thought would most interest Maddie.

"We'll go to the exhibits of Fiji, Samoa and New Zealand," he said. "We'll come here again before you go home, and you can see what we miss today."

They watched the students demonstrate the culture respective to their native islands through song, dance, display of musical instruments and samples of their craft and food. After walking from one site to another, Maddie was ready for the restful canoe ride around the whole area. Although the center was crowded with hundreds of tourists, she and Linc didn't know any of them. She felt as if they were in a world of their own,

For dinner, Linc bought tickets to attend Ali'i Luau.

"You won't think much of Everyday Luau after you attend this," he joked. "This is reportedly Hawaii's largest and most authentic luau. I don't want you to miss it."

And Maddie was glad she hadn't. When they walked through the gates, she felt as if she'd been plunged into the past. The attendant gave her an orchid lei, which Linc placed over the shell lei she'd received at the gate. People representing King Kamehameha, the king who unified Hawaii in the late eighteenth century, and his court entertained the guests with ceremonial songs and dances.

Flickering tiki lamps and waterfalls contributed to Maddie's sensation that she had boarded a time-travel rocket that had catapulted Linc and her back two hundred years. The food didn't differ much from the food served in Linc's restaurants, but the ancient atmosphere appealed to Maddie. But she told Linc loyally that his reproduction of the luau was as good as the real thing.

After Maddie remained silent for half the return drive, Linc said, "Are you sleepy?"

"No, not much. I've enjoyed today very much, but I thought some of the rituals were very frightening. They brought to mind some unpleasant things I read about the early history of the islands. As we watched the ancient rites, I could almost believe that some of the traditions have carried over to the present."

"There is a lot of superstition among the people," Linc agreed, "but being an outsider, I've never paid any attention to it. What did you read?"

"About the custom of sacrificing prisoners taken in battle. The priest slaughtered them outside the temple walls, and the bodies were left to decay on the altars. The left eye of a victim was often given to the king."

"But those things happened hundreds of years ago."

His words did little to reassure her. "Sometimes to celebrate a victory in battle, or even the construction of an altar or temple, the altars were heaped with human bodies. One account indicated that a few tribes carry on these traditions."

"Don't worry about it," Linc said soothingly. "Such customs might still be practiced among some of the people in the isolated mountains, but I doubt it happens in the more populous areas."

It was past midnight when they arrived home, and Linc walked Maddie to the cottage.

"I've asked Roselina to prepare breakfast by seven tomorrow morning, if that isn't too early for you. We'll go to Kauai first and overnight there. I intend to stay two nights on the island of Hawaii. You may not see all you want to in three days, but since you'll be here for a month, we can go back after Christmas."

Maddie took the key from her purse, and opened the guesthouse door. She turned to him. "I feel badly that you're spending so much money on me. Not only have you paid for my plane ticket from home, you're taking me to expensive restaurants, and now you're planning more flights. Please let me pay for my own hotel bills and plane tickets while I'm here."

He leaned against the corner of the cottage door. "Of course not. I have my own plane, and I fly back and forth to the islands, just like you'd drive around your state in a car."

"You own a plane? You're the pilot?"

He laughed at her. "I learned to fly in the navy. The plane is a small four-seater. You won't be afraid to fly with me, will you?" he teased.

"No. I've heard it's safer than driving in a car."

"You're afraid of my driving?" he said, his eyebrows lifting.

She shook her head. "You're trying to distract me. You're spending too much money on me," she insisted.

When she'd shaken her head, a long blond wave had fallen over her shoulder. He lifted the soft tresses and sifted them softly through his fingers.

"Don't you think I've enjoyed the past two days as much as you have?"

Maddie lowered her eyes, thankful for the dim light, because she felt her cheeks getting rosy. "You've seemed to," she murmured.

"Then don't try to deny me the pleasure of entertaining you. I invited you to come to Hawaii because I want to introduce you to the state I've chosen for my home."

"Do you plan to live here for the rest of your life?"

"I don't have ties to any other place. Counting my years in the navy, I've lived in Hawaii for fourteen years. That's longer than I've lived anywhere else. I've prospered in business here. I don't have any plans to leave."

Hawaii seemed even more desirable now that Maddie had come. But how empty would the islands seem, how empty would his home be when she left? In a few days she'd wormed herself into his heart and his life. What would it be like to say goodbye to her when she left Hawaii?

FIVE

Their early morning departure was delayed when Linc received a call before he went to bed from Claudia Warren, a detective with the state police. She was a highly skilled officer, and Linc had met her a few times. Born in Hawaii, Claudia Warren was fortyish, sturdily built with short gray hair. Twenty years of her life had been spent in the service of the Hawaiian State Police.

"I understand you have a guest by the name of Madison Horton," the detective said.

Linc hesitated before he answered. "That's right."

"I need to talk with Miss Horton. Do you want to bring her into our headquarters, or shall I come to your house?"

"We're planning to leave tomorrow morning for a few days of sightseeing. Will it be all right to meet with you after we return?"

"No. I want to see her as soon as possible. I'll come to your home tomorrow morning. Is eight o'clock convenient?"

"Yes."

Linc rested his hand on the phone for several minutes, wondering why the detective needed to see Maddie. He decided against telling her about the detective's visit tonight, because if she knew, she wouldn't sleep. As he undressed for bed, he doubted that he would get any rest. He wanted Maddie's visit to be carefree, but now he wondered if he had made a mistake in inviting her to visit him. He didn't want her to be in danger, yet he couldn't be sorry that Maddie had come into his life.

In spite of his concern, Linc slept, and he felt rested when he woke up. He called Maddie at six o'clock, so she would be ready by the time the detective came. She looked unbelievably lovely and happy when she came for breakfast, and he delayed telling her about the detective's visit until after they had finished eating.

When he told her about his phone call the night before, her startled blue eyes scanned his face quickly.

"Do you know why she wants to see me?"

He shook his head. "I didn't ask."

"I'm scared."

"No need to get scared until we hear what she has to say."

Linc was pleased to see the detective arrive in an unmarked car, so it wouldn't be obvious to the neighbors that a police officer had come to the house. He met Claudia at the door, shook hands with her and directed her into the living room where Maddie sat on the edge of the divan.

Claudia pulled a chair close to Maddie and took her hand. Her motherly attitude eased Maddie's apprehension, but she still must have looked frightened, because the detective said, "There's no need to be afraid of me."

Maddie did feel calmer, but she was annoyed that the detective was treating her like a child.

Claudia Warren turned to Linc. "I need to know why Miss Horton is in Hawaii at this particular time, and how much she knows about her father's death."

Linc explained his connection with Maddie's family in concise terms, ending with, "I told her yesterday about the suspicion now related to her father's death."

"Very good," Claudia Warren said. "We have learned that the Sanale family has more or less declared a vendetta against Horton's relatives. It took us a while, but we finally traced Miss Horton to VOH, and the director, Caroline Renault, told us that she was in Hawaii visiting you."

"More importantly," Linc said, "who else knows that she is here?"

"I don't know. I'm not suggesting that you go into hiding, Miss Horton, but we wanted you to know that you have an enemy at large in the area. Mainly, just be careful and keep a low profile on your visit." Turning to Linc, she said, "We won't insist on police protection now, but if you see anything suspicious, you should report it to me."

After the detective left, Linc said, "We'll continue our plans as though this hasn't happened."

"Actually, I feel safer now that I know the police are aware that I'm in Hawaii," Maddie admitted.

"And so do I. Get your things ready, and we'll leave soon."

The red-and-white small plane stood in front of the hangar that Linc rented at a private airport. To Maddie, the plane looked like a toy when she compared it to the Boeing jet she'd taken from Houston to Hawaii.

Linc parked his auto, picked up his luggage and Maddie's, and they walked to his plane. A mechanic came out of the small office building.

"All gassed up and ready to go, Mr. Carey. We gave the plane the annual checkup yesterday. It's in tip-top shape. Hard to believe the plane is over twenty years old, and good for a lot more years. They don't make 'em like this anymore."

"Thanks, Amos."

The mechanic's words encouraged Maddie a little, and when she stood under the wings of the small plane, she realized it was bigger than she thought. Linc stowed their luggage on the backseat, and pulled the front right seat backward to give her room to enter.

"Put your foot on the little step." He pointed out a narrow step near the ground. Indicating the upper side of the door, he added, "Grab this handle and pull yourself up."

He took her arm. Maddie held her breath, but she followed his instructions. After she was settled in the seat, he closed the door. Automatically, Maddie reached for her seat belt and was buckled in when Linc climbed into the plane from the other side.

The cockpit was narrow, and their shoulders touched when he sat beside her. His nearness calmed her nerves somewhat. The panel in front of her resembled an automobile's, although there were a lot more gadgets than in her car.

Linc turned knobs, checked the radio and talked to the tower.

"I trust the mechanics," he said, "but I double-check everything before I take off." He tugged on a wavy tress of hair that hung over her shoulder. "Especially when I have such a special passenger today."

His words pleased Maddie. It was his tone she didn't like. Linc explained about the operation of the plane, most of which she didn't understand, and ended by saying, "It's easier to fly a plane than to drive a car, so don't be afraid. You'll soon feel at ease."

Linc turned the keys in the ignition, the propeller started rotating and the engine roared. They waited for two other planes to land. Receiving permission from the tower to take off, he taxied to the runway. The bottom of the wings was eye level with Maddie, but she had a good view.

After more two-way communication with the tower, Linc gunned the engine and started forward. Maddie grabbed the arms of her seat, closed her eyes and prayed. She felt like a bird when the plane lifted from the runway, but she couldn't open her eyes.

Still busy checking the weather and wind velocity, Linc didn't pay much attention to Maddie. When he did look in her direction, he stifled a shout of laughter. Her eyes were clamped so tight, he wondered if she'd ever be able to open them. Her fingers had turned white from gripping the steering yoke so tightly.

When he had the plane balanced to his satisfaction, Linc touched her shoulder. She jumped and released her breath in one big surge.

"We're in the air and everything is great."

She blinked one eye experimentally, then opened the other one. "I'm sorry," she said, "but it's such a little plane, and there's a big ocean below us."

Suddenly she noticed that he had one hand on her shoulder, and the other hand was adjusting something on the panel.

"Oh, don't take your hands off the steering wheel," she said, and her eyes closed again.

"Relax," Linc said. "As long as the plane is balanced correctly, and it is, it can take care of itself. And it's called a steering yoke, not a wheel."

She turned loose the yoke in front of her as if it were was a hot potato. "Maybe I shouldn't be holding on to this."

"No reason not to," he said. "You can fly the plane if you want to."

Leaning back in her seat as far as she could go, she lifted her hands. "Oh, no."

Not paying any attention to her denial, he said. "It's simple. You drive a car, don't you?"

She nodded.

"Okay. You turn the yoke to the right or left, whichever direction you want to take. It takes very little pressure to do that. If you want the plane to go down, you push the yoke in. If you want it to go up, pull back on the wheel." He demonstrated the moves as he talked. "You'll soon get used to it. I'll have you guiding the plane before long."

To Maddie, it seemed as if the plane was going very slow, almost suspended in air. "How fast are we going?"

"About a hundred ten miles an hour. And I'm flying at an altitude of twenty-four hundred feet so you can have a good view of the area."

His matter-of-fact tone as he talked about the plane did calm Maddie, and she looked out the window. The shadow of the plane drifted along with them. She could easily discern small fishing boats and some large commercial boats below. They flew over small, uninhabited islands, and Linc explained there were one hundred thirty-two islands in the chain.

The flight to Kauai took less than an hour, and because the smaller plane could fly at a lower altitude than the jet she'd taken into Honolulu, Maddie got a better understanding of the ocean and the islands. After they landed at Lihue, Linc rented a car and drove several miles to a marina to catch a boat for a ride on the Wailua River.

Linc and Maddie were the first to board the red-and-white boat, which resembled a covered barge with wooden seats around the periphery of the craft. Linc chose seats in the back, which would give Maddie the best view. A man and woman, dressed in traditional Hawaiian garments, came on board. The man carried a ukulele, and Maddie turned to Linc, smiling in contentment because she sat beside him, knowing he shared her enjoyment of each new thing she experienced.

"They'll provide live music while we travel," he said.

Maddie's eyes brightened with merriment when a large group approached the barge. A woman boarded, wearing a wedding dress and holding the arm of a man wearing a tux. They were followed by several other people, presumably their relatives. All members of the party wore white orchid leis.

"Our destination is the Fern Grotto, and it's a popular place for weddings," Linc explained quietly. "Couples from all over the world come here to be married. The easiest access to the grotto is by boat."

As soon as the wedding party settled into their seats, and a few other passengers came aboard, the pilot hustled down the wooden steps into the barge. He backed the boat into the current and headed upstream. Interspersed with the traditional Hawaiian songs of the musicians, a male guide stood beside the pilot, commenting on the scenery. Until his narration, Maddie hadn't realized that the vegetation they saw was among the most abundant subtropical vegetation in the world.

The river was lined with lush-foliaged trees with

branches sweeping the water. Canoes glided down-river. A few tents were set up along an occasional sandy beach.

Maddie had read that Kauai was the oldest island in the Hawaiian chain and that a single volcano had made the island. When the guide spoke of ancient Kauai chieftains who'd once lived in this valley, Maddie shuddered at his vivid descriptions of the harsh justice the natives meted out to their enemies.

When they landed at the wharf near the grotto, a man, presumably the father of the bride, invited all of the passengers to attend the wedding ceremony.

His mouth curving with tenderness, Linc said, "I assume you want to watch the wedding."

"Why, yes. Don't you?"

"I wouldn't miss it."

Linc had attended other weddings at the grotto, but he welcomed this opportunity to observe Maddie's reaction to the romantic atmosphere.

Glancing at Maddie's sandals, Linc said, "I should have told you to wear walking shoes. There's a lot of rain on this island, and the walk uphill to the grotto is always slippery. The path is narrow, so we'll have to walk single file most of the way. Be careful. I'll walk behind you if you need any help."

They wound uphill through ferns and vines that had intertwined with tall, broad-leaved trees. The area reminded Maddie of a film she'd seen of tropical jungles. She gathered that dwellings must be located nearby for numerous cats played in the woods, and she heard roosters crowing.

Fern Grotto was a large, obscure cave with lush vines hanging over the opening. Maddie wondered if the sun ever shone directly into the deep hollow. Steady streams of water dripped from the ledge that formed a roof over the spot where the wedding party assembled.

Several rows of bleachers had been cut into a natural stone wall on the ledge below the grotto. Linc and Maddie left the seats for the wedding party. They leaned against a large tree and listened to the prenuptial music presented by the musicians from the boat. They played traditional wedding melodies and sang softly while the minister and the bridal party moved into place on the level above the guests.

The acoustics were good in the glen, and Maddie easily heard the words of the wedding service. At the close, the musicians sang the Hawaiian Wedding Song, first in Hawaiian and then in English. The music was familiar to Maddie, and she closed her eyes, humming the tune and thinking of the words.

She opened her eyes and was startled when she saw a brawny, squat Hawaiian standing nearby staring at her. The malevolence in his eyes was frightening. She turned away and moved close to Linc, who apparently saw the fright in her eyes, for he put his arm around her shoulders.

"What's wrong?" he asked.

"That man—staring at me," she said, lifting her

head to point to the man, but he was gone. "Oh, he isn't there now. He looked like the same man who stared at me in the Everyday Luau restaurant. He's a big man with broad features."

Linc didn't once consider that Maddie was the kind of person to imagine such a thing, and he scanned the group of guests. He couldn't see anyone matching the description Maddie had given, although he thought he heard someone plunging downward through the heavy vines and trees. Maddie's blond beauty was bound to attract a lot of attention, and the man probably meant no harm. It was unlikely that this was the same man Maddie had noticed in Honolulu. He'd heard many an outsider say that all Hawaiian men looked the same to them, and that may have contributed to the mistaken identity.

"Don't worry about it now," he said. "Do you want to climb to the grotto and greet the bride and groom? You can get a better sense of the enormity of the grotto when you're inside it."

Eyeing the slick upward path, Maddie said, "I'd like to go, but I'm afraid to try it in these sandals."

"I'll help you," he said. "I'll go ahead and you can hold my hand. I won't let you slip."

Her eye contact with the stranger had caused her heart to pound with an accompanying physical weakness, but holding on to Linc's hand, she made the ascent without a problem.

Although he kept warning himself to stop considering impossible scenarios, Linc was interested in Maddie's reaction to the grotto as a site for a wedding. He'd often thought that if he ever married, he would like to have the ceremony in that spot.

Long vines hung from the top of the cave. Water dripped from the grotto's overhang, and it seemed to Maddie that she was peering through a bead curtain. Linc still held her hand when they were on level ground for the grotto's floor was wet.

"I don't know how she walked up those steps in that long wedding dress," she murmured quietly. "If I were planning a wedding here, I'd choose a simple dress with a short skirt."

"When you get married, would you want a traditional wedding at home, or a simple ceremony like this?" Linc asked.

Not daring to look at him, Maddie peered into the rugged gully below them. "I haven't thought about my wedding a whole lot, but there does seem to be an aura of romance in this place."

They chatted with members of the wedding party and learned that the bride and groom were from California. Maddie took a few pictures of the grotto before they went back to the river.

Maddie was very quiet as they sat on a bench until it was time to board the boat. Linc had noted that she wasn't a chatterer, but she was usually full of questions when he took her to a new place. Not only was she silent now, but she peered intently at everyone who passed them.

"Are you still worried about the guy who stared at you?"

"A little, I guess."

Not knowing how much he dared to say, Linc asked in a teasing manner, "Haven't you looked in the mirror enough to realize why people stare at you?"

Startled blue eyes met his. She lifted a hand to her face. "What do you mean? What's wrong with my face?"

"Nothing. Nothing at all," he hurriedly reassured. "But don't you realize that a blond beauty like you is a vivid contrast to what people on the islands are accustomed to seeing? They naturally take a second look."

"I've seen other blondes here."

"That's true," he agreed, amazed that Maddie wasn't aware of the extent of her beauty. "Many blondes live in Hawaii, but you don't seem to realize that you're beautiful."

Maddie dropped her eyes in confusion. "My friends, Janice and Lucy, often tease me about being Miss Model or Miss Movie Star. But I didn't take it seriously because, during the two years I spent at VOH, Miss Caroline indoctrinated all of us with the principle that beauty is more than skin deep. She wanted us to develop an inner spiritual beauty, the kind that would last when youthful beauty faded."

"I didn't intend to embarrass you, but I wanted you to realize that the man may have been startled by your beauty. Don't let your fear spoil our day."

Maddie had often thought that her good looks were a curse instead of a blessing, especially after she'd gone to college. She'd attracted the attention of men, whom she wouldn't date, because she figured they wanted to go out with her for the wrong reasons. Also, she'd been chided by a few people who thought you couldn't be intelligent and beautiful, too. More than once, she'd been called a "dumb blonde." After carrying a perfect grade point average the first year at the university, she hadn't heard that accusation as much.

When the boat got underway for the return journey, Maddie asked, "Wouldn't it cost a lot of money to come here from California for a wedding?"

"I doubt it's much more than the cost of a formal wedding on the mainland. Many people from the western states honeymoon in Hawaii. And a lot of Asian residents come here for weddings, too. It's especially popular to be married in the Fern Grotto and on Waikiki beach. Companies have package deals that cater to the wishes of each couple, a traditional wedding in a church or choose a less formal ceremony. Older couples often come here for special anniversaries to renew their vows."

"I suppose I shouldn't ask this, but why haven't you gotten married?" Maddie asked. She thought, but didn't say, that she couldn't imagine anyone who wouldn't want to marry him. "Living in such a romantic place, I'd have thought, at your age, you would have married."

Wincing a little at the words, *at your age,* without looking at her, Linc answered, "For two reasons, really. I've been so busy establishing and expanding my restaurants that I haven't taken time for romance. Also, I suppose I'm an idealist, but I don't want to get married until I find that special person I can't live without."

"And you haven't found her?" she inquired in wide-eyed innocence.

Fortunately for Linc, the boat's pilot announced that they would be docking in ten minutes. The best man walked through the barge handing all the passengers bags of birdseed to be thrown at the bride and groom as they left the boat.

Linc was spared an answer that he didn't dare to give, and Maddie was left in doubt and confusion. Had he found that special person in Ahonui, and he didn't want to tell her?

SIX

As they returned to the city of Lihue, where Linc had reserved rooms for the night, he asked, "Would you like to go shopping now? We'll pass a big store with all kinds of native products."

She slanted an amused glance toward him. "Men don't like to shop, do they?"

"I'm sure I'll enjoy watching you shop." Actually, he wanted to find out what interested Maddie, so he'd know what to buy her for Christmas. If he learned her tastes, he could do his shopping later when she wasn't along.

"I do want to buy some Hawaiian clothes," Maddie said. "But I don't want to spend much money."

"This store features items in a wide range of prices. Let's stop and you can take a look." He drove into the parking lot of a vast metal building that looked like a warehouse.

"I'll look for a dress and a shirt to wear while I'm here. I intend to buy some souvenirs for my friends before I go home. I can get an idea of what's available and buy them later."

The vast array of merchandise overwhelmed Maddie, and for two hours they wended their way through the store, so crowded with tourists and merchandise that it was impossible to hurry. Maddie chose a sleeveless dress in a blue print that matched her eyes, and a colorful shirt with palm trees on it. Linc bought a shirt to match hers.

"We can wear these when we go out to dinner," Linc said, and Maddie wondered if there was anything significant in the fact that he wanted a shirt identical to hers. When Maddie went to try on her dress and shirt, Linc bought a black pearl necklace and matching earrings, thinking how lovely they would look on Maddie's ivory skin. He took the package to the car before she returned.

Maddie's pleasure in the shopping expedition suffered a setback when they left the store. The man who'd watched her at the Fern Grotto was stepping out of a car not ten feet from where she stood. She gasped, but before she could call Linc's attention to the man, he ducked around the corner.

Since Linc had treated the previous incident lightly, she didn't say anything, for she didn't want him to think she was paranoid. At the hotel, they changed into their matching shirts before they went out. Maddie tried to keep a stiff upper lip during the rest of the evening while they took a walking tour of

Lihue and ate dinner at a Chinese restaurant. But she couldn't forget the man who'd been watching her.

She slept fitfully, and in her dreams, she kept seeing his face. His black eyes seemed to spell trouble for her. In the dream, everywhere she went, the man followed her, and once he confronted her with an uplifted knife. She woke up, calling for Linc to help her, but of course, he couldn't hear in his room across the hall.

They left Kauai early the next morning for the flight to Hilo, the county seat of the big island of Hawaii. Again, Linc rented a car, and they spent most of the day driving around the island. In a guide-book, Maddie had read that agriculture contributed largely to the island's economy. Linc pointed out large sugar plantations, cattle ranches, vegetable farms, orchid nurseries and orchards that produced coffee plants, macadamia nuts and fruits.

They spent a few hours in Volcano National Park before returning to spend the night in a deluxe resort hotel.

"You'll like what we're going to see today," Linc said the next morning as they left the hotel after a buffet breakfast. Maddie was still concerned about the money Linc was spending. The rates posted in her hotel rooms distressed her. She didn't want him to think she expected so much attention. But since she was convinced he was enjoying their time together as much as she was, she didn't spoil their companionship by harping on the money he spent.

"We're going to a national park that features aspects of traditional Hawaiian life," Linc explained as they wound through the hilly land in a rented car with the coastline often in sight. "At one time this area was the residence of royal chieftains, and close by is a place of refuge with historical significance. I think you'll enjoy it."

"I've enjoyed everything we've done over the past week. It doesn't seem possible that I've seen so much in such a few days. I don't know how to thank you."

"You're thanking me by having a good time. This is the first time I've shown anyone around the islands on their first visit. It's the best vacation I've had for years."

"Where do you usually go on vacations?"

"It's no fun vacationing alone, so I combine my vacations with business trips. I go to California, China and Japan often."

Since Maddie had enjoyed Hawaii so much, Linc wished that he could show her the wonders of the Orient.

Pu'uhonua o Hōnaunau was located in a barren area along the seacoast. The royal grounds were separated from the place of refuge by a massive wall. Linc and Maddie took a self-guided tour of the place of refuge, moving from exhibit to exhibit as Maddie read from the guidebook. She had a gentle voice, soft and clear. Through her eyes, Linc appreciated more than ever the history of his chosen state.

"The pu'uhonua was a place of refuge for defeated warriors, noncombatants in time of war, or those who violated the sacred laws," Maddie read. "When a sacred law was broken the penalty was always death. Otherwise the gods might react violently, perhaps with volcanic eruptions, tidal waves, famines or earthquakes. The lawbreaker would be put to death unless he reached the place of refuge."

They spent an hour sauntering among the exhibits which illustrated many facets of ancestral Hawaiian culture. Black volcanic rocks were scattered along the beach. Towering palm trees added interest to the site. They paused to observe the numerous turtles crawling in the shallow water.

As they looked at several tall wooden carvings, Maddie said, "These remind me of the Native American totem poles of our Northwest." She pointed to a man hollowing out a log to make a boat. "And that's very similar to the dugout canoes of the Eastern Indians."

"I've always noticed the similarity between residents of these islands and mainland aborigines," Linc agreed.

The coastline was marked by stunted trees. After they inspected the stockade-protected sanctuary for those who needed mercy, Linc stopped beside a bench shaded by a coconut palm. "Let's sit and rest before we move on. I've got sand in my shoes."

He took off his tennis shoes and shook out the sand, then leaned against the back of the bench, looking out over the water with contentment mirrored on his face.

Maddie continued to be amazed that a man, who must have a lot of work to do, seemed in no hurry at all. They sat, shoulders touching, and Maddie gazed at the inlet separating the place of refuge from the rugged hills on the other side of the water. The inlet was shallow now, but at high tide, there would be a large wall of water. If a warrior was wounded or weary from being pursued, how vulnerable, how scared he must have been when he faced the last barrier between death and freedom.

Linc watched the play of emotions on Maddie's face as she stared across the cove for at least ten minutes without saying a word. He placed his hand on her shoulder, and she jumped.

"I didn't mean to startle you," he apologized. "Do you want to share your thoughts?"

"I was thinking about the people who came seeking shelter here. It must have been a frightful experience for them. Imagine how grateful they would have been when their feet touched this side of the coast and they knew that they were safe."

"I wouldn't have wanted to live in ancient times," Linc said.

"No," Maddie agreed. "Especially since the islanders didn't know about the refuge they could find in Christ Jesus. When did Christianity come to the islands?"

"In the early nineteenth century. I don't remember

the exact year. The missionaries worked many years before the Christian faith was widespread. As I told you earlier, there are still groups who adhere to the old religions—especially those who worship the volcano gods. They give gifts to the gods to protect them from danger. In earlier times, human sacrifices were made, but thankfully that's no longer true."

Maddie remembered her dreams in the hotel of Kauai, and she shuddered. Still she knew she didn't have to fear her enemies when God was her refuge.

For self-assurance, she said, "When Jesus died on the cross, He provided a place of refuge for everyone." She reached in her tote bag and drew out a New Testament. "Do you mind if I look up a Scripture passage that reminds me of this place? I can't seem to remember it completely."

"Not at all," he said. "Read it aloud."

Maddie flipped to the book of Hebrews, scanned the sixth chapter and found the verses. "The writer was encouraging his readers to put their confidence in God's promises to protect His followers. Oh, here's the verse I've been thinking about. 'We who have fled to take hold of the hope offered to us may be greatly encouraged. We have this hope as an anchor for the soul, firm and secure.'"

Still musing on the past customs of the Hawaiians, her subconscious thoughts surfaced. "I couldn't have emotionally survived the deaths of my parents if I hadn't been confident that God had prepared a home for them. They passed safely from this world to the next one because Jesus had already provided a refuge for them."

"I've often thought about the Scripture the minister read at your father's funeral," Linc said. "After I returned to Hawaii, I looked it up in the Bible and committed it to memory."

"Would you say it, please? I think of my parents every time I hear those words."

"'Let not your heart be troubled; you believe in God, believe also in Me. In My Father's house are many mansions: if it were not so, I would have told you. I go to prepare a place for you. And if I go to prepare a place for you, I will come again, and receive you unto Myself; that where I am there you may be also.'"

"I asked for the same Scripture to be read at Mother's funeral," Maddie said. A tender expression crossed her face as she thought of her parents.

"Those days must have been difficult for you," Linc said compassionately. "How old were you when your mother died?"

"Sixteen. But Mother knew she was dying, and we talked about what I should do. She made arrangements for me to spend the next two years with Miss Caroline at the Valley of Hope. Miss Caroline helped me realize that the hope I had in Christ Jesus would be a firm, steadfast hope throughout my life."

Linc had admired Maddie's poised, erect stance from the first day, for she carried herself with dignity. Now her shoulders slumped despairingly as she recalled the deaths of her parents. Linc wanted to put a comforting arm around her shoulders, but he resisted the impulse.

Instead he focused on the things Maddie had said. He had once possessed the kind of faith Maddie exemplified. When his parents had died, and he'd joined the navy, instead of remaining secure in the hope he had, he'd wandered away from the childhood commitment he'd made to serve God. Sitting there with Maddie by his side, he felt as if he was again in the little church where he'd surrendered his life and will to God. He reached for Maddie's hand, bowed his head and prayed quietly.

"God, forgive me for straying. I'm a runaway needing a sanctuary. Take me back into that refuge today, and I promise I'll never leave Your presence again."

Maddie squeezed his hand and lifted it to her lips. Her eyes filled with tears when she turned her luminous gaze toward him.

"That was beautiful," she said. "I feel as if we're standing on holy ground, and that God is very near to us."

Throwing caution aside, Linc hugged her to him and, in bliss too deep for words she rested her head on his shoulder.

But as they stood to leave, Maddie looked again across the water. In her mind's eye, she saw a fugitive running toward the shore. When the hunted person paused on the beach before plunging into the raging water, it was her own face she saw on the fugitive. She gasped, her face whitened, and Linc's protective arm again encircled her shoulders.

"What is it?" he said, alarmed.

Her lips trembled, and she told him her thoughts. "I have too vivid an imagination," she said.

"Forget about it," Linc said soothingly. "You're just upset because of Detective Warren's visit. Remember you've already found a Place of Refuge. You have nothing to fear." He kept his arm around her as they returned to the administration building of the park.

She knew he was right, and her mood lightened, but she couldn't put the incident out of her mind. Maddie glanced through a few pamphlets while Linc brought the car from the parking area. Suddenly she had the uncanny feeling that she was being watched, and she looked quickly behind her. A woman stood at the corner of the building. Maddie only had time to note how much she resembled the man who'd been stalking her before the woman dodged out of sight.

Not wanting to spoil Linc's experience of renewing his faith, Maddie got in the car without mentioning the woman. It had to be a coincidence. Maybe people *were* staring at her because her appearance was so different from most of Hawaii's residents. She reminded herself that she did have a steadfast hope that was promised to her forever. Now Linc had the same confidence—hope that they both needed when they returned to Honolulu and encountered a situation that neither of them had anticipated.

SEVEN

Ahonui hadn't left any messages on his phone, so Linc hadn't called the office for the past three days. He had wondered if she was pouting because he hadn't told her where he'd be, or whether there hadn't been any need to contact him. But now that their journey was over, he was eager to find out what had happened while they were away. He taxied the plane into his private hangar, picked up his car and they headed for home.

Roselina waved to them from the front veranda when they arrived. For a moment, Maddie felt as if she was home, too. That was wishful thinking, for it had been four years since she'd actually had a home.

Since Linc intended to go to the office, he stopped the car in front of the house.

Roselina came to the car. "I've missed you," she said. "You want anything to eat now?"

"We had a late breakfast in Kona," Linc said. "I won't need anything to eat until dinner, but Maddie may be hungry."

"Oh, no," she protested. "I've been eating too much the past few days. But we had a wonderful time, Roselina. I want to do some laundry. Is it all right to use the washer and dryer in the cottage?"

"Sure. There's everything you need."

"I'll go to the office and see what's been happening the past few days," Linc said. "To tell the truth, I'm not eager to go back to work—I could soon get accustomed to being lazy."

"Trouble with you, Mr. Linc, you work too much. I'm glad Miss Maddie is here to see that you have a little fun."

Linc carried Maddie's luggage to the cottage and deposited it on the floor when she opened the door.

"I'll see you tonight," he said, loathe to leave her for a few hours.

"Thanks, again," Maddie said, and Linc wondered at the unreadable message in her eyes.

Roselina waited for Linc when he returned to the house, and the expression on her face was a harbinger of bad news. She handed him the morning newspaper. It was a small article but a disturbing one.

Stanley Horton's daughter visits Hawaii. Madison Horton, daughter of Stanley Horton, whose death is now being investigated as a homicide, is visiting in Hawaii at this time. Kamu Sanale, wanted for questioning about

Horton's death, is still at large. Is there any connection between the arrival of Miss Horton and the prison escape?

A picture of Sanale was inserted in the article.

Linc had hoped he could keep Maddie's name from being connected to this investigation, for he didn't want reporters pestering her. Who had leaked this news? He didn't believe that the police would have given out the information.

"Don't show this to Maddie yet," he said to Roselina. "I don't know how the papers got this information, but I may learn something at the office. I'll be back by dinnertime."

How had the press found out about Maddie's visit? The question rolled back and forth in Linc's mind during the drive into the city. If his suspicions were correct, he considered the best way to deal with the situation.

Ahonui was out to lunch when he got to the office, so Linc busied himself with messages left on his answering machine. Ahonui always screened his mail and disposed of messages that weren't of interest to him, so he didn't have as much correspondence on his desk as he'd feared he might have. He had finished with the mail when she returned.

"I've missed you. Did you have a pleasant trip? I suppose Maddie enjoyed seeing new places."

Linc was reluctant to discuss Maddie with anyone, so he simply said, "Yes, we had a good trip."

He indicated some envelopes he'd laid aside. "There doesn't seem to be much pending—except these two letters that need to be answered. I'll record my reply and you can take care of them tomorrow morning."

"Aren't you coming to work tomorrow?"

He lifted his eyebrows. "Yes, I intend to, but I don't know what time I'll be here, and I want these letters in the early mail. I'm interviewing three men for the position of manager of the new restaurant that will open in two months. I wouldn't forget that."

"Oh, I don't know. You missed an appointment two days ago."

"One that I canceled from Kauai. How did the press learn that Maddie is visiting me?"

She had started toward her office, but she swung around. "I didn't tell them if that's what you're suggesting!"

"You *did* see the article in the paper about her?"

"Not until Steve called it to my attention."

He believed her, but if she hadn't done it, who had? How many people knew that Maddie was visiting him? Roselina for one, but he was sure she hadn't said anything. Steve was a possibility, but what reason could he have to mention the visit? Who else even knew she was in the islands?

The church congregation! Of course. There were fifty or more people at the worship service last Sunday. He knew only a few of them, but it was quite possible that one of them knew about Maddie's connection to the escaped felons. Whoever had spread the news could have done it innocently.

Ahonui tossed her head impatiently, and he knew she was angry.

"I'm sorry I doubted you," Linc said sincerely. "I thought only a few people knew that Maddie was here, but I guess there are others."

"Everyone in this office knows. And you can't go away for three days without a lot of people knowing you're gone. And before she came, you told the office staff about your little friend's visit and that you'd served in the navy with her father."

He shrugged his shoulders. "I guess I did."

"But for her own safety, don't you think it's time she went home?"

"It may come to that, but I'll wait a little while."

"Just be sure you don't wait too long," Ahonui said, and her words sounded like a warning to Linc.

As he drove home, Linc decided that he must tell Maddie about the article connecting her name with the prison escape. He put the car in the garage, got the newspaper out of the house and walked to the cottage. He heard Maddie singing above the noise of the washer and dryer. She had a clear, mellow contralto voice. He pecked on the door.

The singing stopped and Maddie came from the bedroom alcove. "Hi," she said. "The door's open. Come in."

"I heard you singing. You have a beautiful voice."

She blushed prettily. "Oh, I don't know how beautiful it is, but Miss Caroline always said that we should glorify God with our voices. I like to sing. My friend, Janice Reid, and I often sang duets for worship service when we were both at VOH."

He still stood by the door, and Maddie said, "Is there anything wrong?"

"I don't know," he said. She eyed him uneasily.

"Sit down," she invited, adding with a smile, "Can I serve you a glass of your own cola?"

"That would be fine. I am thirsty."

While she rustled around filling two glasses with ice and opening a can of cola, which she divided between the two glasses, he wondered how to break the news. He thanked her for the drink and perched on a stool at the breakfast bar. He handed her the paper, with the article displayed.

"I hoped it wouldn't become widespread knowledge that you were visiting the islands."

She read the article, choking back a frightened cry. The fear mirrored in her eyes made her look like a cornered animal.

"Maybe that's the man who's been stalking me," she stammered. "I thought he was watching me at the national park, too, but I didn't tell you for that person turned out to be a woman rather than a man. I suppose it was my imagination that she looked like the man."

Linc turned the page and pointed to the picture of the felon who had escaped. "Does this look like the man you've seen?"

It was heartening to Maddie that Linc didn't seem to question her word. At times *she* even wondered if she was imagining the stalker. "Maybe, but I don't know. I've just had a few fleeting looks at him, and most of the natives look alike to me. Do you think I'm in danger?"

"I hope not, but perhaps you'd better go home."

Maddie felt as if he'd thrown a pan of cold water in her face. "Do you want me to leave?"

"Of course not, but I do want you to be safe. I feel responsible for you."

Maddie didn't want to be considered a responsibility. Tears stung her eyes and she turned away from him, but not before he noticed her trembling lips.

"Go ahead and arrange my flight. I'll pack my clothes." Without looking at him, she walked into the bathroom and closed the door.

Feeling like a cad, Linc left the cottage and went to the house. Roselina was running the sweeper in the living room. She turned off the sweeper and rewound the cord.

"What time do you want to eat?"

"I don't know. I suggested to Maddie that it might be wise for her to go home. I'll call the airport to see when I can arrange a flight for her."

Taking the liberty of a longtime employee, she

put her hands on her hips and glared at him. "Why'd you do that?"

"With that convict running loose, I'm afraid for her to stay here."

"If he's after her, he can find her no matter where she is. We can watch over her. She might be as safe here as anywhere."

"Maybe you're right, but I want to do what's best for her," Linc said hesitantly. His heart felt as if it weighed a ton, just considering Maddie's departure. He knew he was grasping at straws to keep her.

"I don't know what is best, but you'd ought to let her make the decision." And looking at him pointedly, she said, "She's not a child, you know, although it's plain that's the way you're treating her."

"I'll go talk to her," he said without commenting on Roselina's insinuation. His housekeeper had the uncanny habit of reading his mind.

His eager steps took him to the cottage quickly. Maddie was taking her clothes from the dryer and hanging them on a rack. Tears were glistening on her cheeks. Since she hadn't seen him, he backed away and approached the door again, making sure he made enough noise that she would hear his approach.

The tears had been wiped from her face when she turned to face him.

"Is it all right if I come in again?" he said, and she nodded.

"Roselina bawled me out. She thinks I'm taking

this situation too seriously. She says you're the one to make the decision about whether to go home or not."

Her face was colorless, and she said stiffly, "I don't consider that's the case. I'm here as your guest and at your expense—you certainly have the right to tell me when to leave."

Linc didn't know whether he'd made her mad, or if he had hurt her feelings. Either way, a warning voice whispered in his head that he would have to exercise caution in smoothing out his mistake. Although he'd been out of the habit of praying for years, Linc silently petitioned, *God, give me the right words and the right attitude.*

He walked close to her, but she stood with her face downcast. He touched her chin and lifted her face. Her long lashes fluttered downward, shielding her eyes.

"Will you believe that my suggestion was made with only your good in mind? I didn't consider my own feelings."

Her lashes lifted slowly. Her eyes searched his face, reaching into his thoughts, and Linc wondered how much she could see. "Then you don't want me to leave?"

He reached for her hands and held them tenderly. "No. But I don't want the same thing to happen to you that happened to your father."

"Do you think there's a possibility of that?"

"I don't know. It's rumored that the Sanale family is connected with an ancient cult that believes in a life-for-life revenge. If they learned you were coming to Hawaii, they might have thought it worthwhile to break out of prison to avenge the death of their father. I don't know that this is true, but it worries me."

"Would it have been common knowledge that I was coming?"

"I wouldn't have thought so. But Ahonui reminded me that all of the people who work for me might have known I'd invited you to visit me. That could be thirty to forty people."

"I don't want to leave. I was looking forward to being in Hawaii for Christmas," Maddie said, "but I shouldn't involve you in my problems. Maybe I should go someplace else. Miss Caroline asked me to check on a friend of hers living in the islands. I could probably stay with her for a few days until we decide what I should do."

"No! If you stay, I want you where I can look after you. After all, since your father is gone, I feel as if I should take his place in protecting you."

The words had been hard to say, and he could tell that he'd hurt her again. But he had to keep a distance between them. He wasn't sure of Maddie's feelings toward him, but the way he felt when he was close to her, she must have experienced some of the same emotions. Suddenly aware that he was still holding her hands, Linc released them quickly and stepped back.

"Thank you," she said stiffly. "I want my father's murderer brought to justice, and hopefully that will be done before I go home."

"Roselina's right and I may be worrying needlessly, but please be cautious. Probably you should call Detective Warren and give her a description of the natives you've seen. In the meantime, I invited you here to enjoy Christmas, and we won't let our worries overshadow that. I have to work for the next two days, but I'll be free over the weekend. Roselina will look after you while I'm at work."

"Thanks for letting me stay," she said.

He left Maddie, still questioning if she should leave Hawaii.

It suited Edena's purpose to have the presence of Madison Horton known to the press. It also pleased her to know that the pale blonde was scared.

After Tivini had learned that Kamu was dead and that he was dealing with a woman, he'd wanted to back out on his agreement to help her. But she'd soon brought him into line. Edena had convinced him that if he double-crossed her, he would be sorry.

Tivini had been helpful in providing a motorboat for Edena to use in scouting the Carey home. They would be surprised to know how many times she'd landed her boat near their beach and had walked through the trees toward the house. Once she'd thought someone had seen her, and she'd run off in a hurry.

She had a net spread around Madison Horton, and when she was ready, she'd trap her like a fish.

EIGHT

The next few days Linc left for work early, and Maddie saw him only at dinner and the rest of the evening. On Thursday, he said, "If you'd like, you can go with me tomorrow, and I'll take you to a library, not far from my office that has a wealth of information on Hawaii's role in World War II."

"Yes, I would like that. I check off the days on the calendar each morning and my vacation time is passing quickly. I'd just as soon get the research done before Christmas. Let's dress in our twin shirts tomorrow."

"I usually wear a suit and tie to work, but it won't break any rules to go in a sport shirt. Actually, we won't be together very much. I'm going to leave you at the library, then pick you up in the afternoon, but we can lunch together. There's a little café near the library."

The next morning when they were ready to start, Maddie came from the guesthouse with a notebook and plenty of pens in her tote.

"Ready?"

"I think I have everything I'll need."

"I've got a laptop in the office. Would you like to use that to take your notes?"

"That would be super. If you don't mind."

"Not at all. Go ahead and settle in the car. I'll bring the laptop and you can check it out as we drive into the city."

Since Maddie had grown up using computers, it wasn't difficult for her to figure out how to use his laptop. She would buy a Zip drive and store the information to transfer to her own computer when she got home.

Linc walked with her into the lobby of the library, which reminded her of the library at WVU. He introduced her to the librarian at the desk, and when she'd been taken to the section containing World War II data, Linc handed her a card with his business phone number.

"Call if you need anything at all. I'll pick you up at one o'clock. We'll have lunch, and I'll take you on a tour of my business offices."

Maddie had an overpowering desire to learn everything she could about Linc, and pleased at his suggestion, she said, "Sounds like a good idea to me."

"If you get hungry before then, there are snack and beverage dispensers in the basement."

"I'll be fine."

The morning hours passed rapidly for Maddie. The library had a comprehensive section on the history of World War II, and she easily singled out the materials she wanted. The library assistants were attentive and showed her anything she couldn't find.

When Linc returned, however, she'd had enough. Her eyes were strained, and her muscles cramped because she'd hunched over the computer for several hours. His eyes brightened with eagerness as they always did when he first saw her after they'd been separated.

"How'd everything go?" he asked as he un-plugged the computer and picked it up.

"Very good. I have all the material I'll need. It's only a short paper—not a thesis."

"It won't be a problem if you need to work here again, but probably not until after Christmas. Roselina wants to start shopping and baking next week."

"Did you get your work finished?"

"Pretty much so. At least enough that I can take a day or two off each week. I'm free for the weekend, but I have to work on Monday."

After they ate a leisurely lunch, Linc hailed a cab that took them to the office. Carey Enterprises occu-pied the whole tenth floor of a high-rise building. He spent an hour showing her everything, and introduc-ing her to his employees. Concern hovered in the back of his mind, and he wondered at the wisdom of having Maddie out in public so much, but what kind of a vacation would it be for her if she had to be cooped up?

Ahonui eyed their matching shirts with a keenly observant eye, but she said nothing about them. The offices were luxurious, and it seemed obvious to Maddie that Linc had a prosperous, substantial business. Ahonui was more cordial to Maddie than usual, and although she watched closely, she couldn't detect any romance between Ahonui and Linc. When Maddie looked back on the day before she went to sleep, she was satisfied with what she'd accomplished.

She thought she'd be lonesome on the days Linc worked, but Roselina kept her so busy that the time passed before she knew it. Roselina liked to talk, and she was obviously happy to have Maddie's company.

"My kids never come here on Christmas because they have little ones," Roselina said on Monday morning when they were alone. "Mr. Linc and I usually spend a quiet time. The last two years, Ahonui and Steve have been with us on Christmas Day because they don't have any other relatives on the islands. They're coming this year, too. But Mr. Linc told me to go all out this year in honor of your visit."

Maddie felt her face coloring when Roselina grinned impudently at her.

"The three of us will have Christmas Eve alone. We'll open presents then, too. I'll let you decide on the foods that appeal to you."

Maddie's optimism dropped a little to know that Ahonui would be with them on Christmas Day. Still, she might as well learn to live with the fact that Linc's only interest in her was as her surrogate father.

"Here's a book of native recipes," Roselina said. "You pick out what you'd like to have. We'll have a buffet meal on Christmas Day, so you can choose more than one meat or whatever you want."

While Roselina prepared to bake two loaves of brown bread and three loaves of pineapple bread, Maddie sat at the kitchen table and, her mouth watering, she leafed through the cookbook.

"This is maddening," she said. "Everything looks good."

Finally, she took a notebook and listed:

For Christmas Eve:
Chicken long rice, sweet and sour green beans, baked bananas, molded tomato salad and Surinam cherry chiffon.

For Christmas Day:
Cabbage soup, Hawaiian shrimp, baked pork, yam bake, cauliflower, water chestnuts and mushrooms cooked together, pasta salad and Harvest Cake.

When Roselina put the last loaves of bread in the oven, she sat at the table. Maddie timidly handed her the list. "Maybe that's too many things and, for all I know, the foods might not complement each other. Don't hesitate to change anything that you want to."

As she read the list, Roselina nodded approvingly. "A good selection."

"I'll help as much as I can."

"The two days before Christmas we'll spend in the kitchen. We'll go shopping for food in a few days, but this afternoon, we'll buy a Christmas tree. We've always used an artificial tree, but Mr. Linc told me this morning to buy a real tree for you."

"I'd rather you wouldn't go to so much trouble for me. I'm not used to a lot of celebrating."

"I do what Mr. Linc wants me to do, but I enjoy having you around. I've never bought a tree, so you'll have to help."

"Are there tree farms on the islands?"

"Norfolk Island pines grow in Hawaii and many people use those. We'll buy a tree flown in from California."

When Roselina took the bread from the oven twenty minutes later, she turned it out on cooling racks.

"We can go shopping now," Roselina said.

Roselina drove a late-model compact car. Because of her diminutive height, she had to stretch to see over the steering wheel, but she was a competent driver. The tree lot was several miles from the house on the outskirts of Honolulu.

It had been a long time since Maddie had helped to buy a Christmas tree. Despite her nostalgic thoughts about the first time her father had taken her to buy a tree, she enjoyed wandering through the rows of evergreens. Roselina didn't like to walk, so she told Maddie to choose what she wanted. After debating for almost an hour, Maddie decided on a ponderosa pine about five feet tall. The manager of the lot tied it on the top of Roselina's car after she paid for the tree.

When they turned to get in the car, a man with a microphone in his hand stepped in front of Maddie. She was suddenly aware that a TV camera was focused on her, and the man thrust the microphone in front of her face.

"Madison Horton?" he said.

"Yes," Maddie mumbled.

"Welcome to Hawaii. Are you enjoying your visit?"

Roselina became aware of what was going on, and she bustled forward just as the reporter said, "Did you come to Hawaii at this time because of the investigation into your father's death?"

"No comment," Roselina said belligerently. "Get in the car, honey."

Roselina stood guard like a Rottweiler until Maddie scooted into the car and locked the door. Roselina hustled into the driver's seat as fast as she could, revved the engine and sped out of the tree lot. The photographer ran beside the car, his camera rolling until Roselina outdistanced him.

"Mr. Linc will have my head for this," Roselina moaned. "He told me to watch out for you."

"How could they know where I'd be?" Maddie asked, realizing a shiver of panic. She was confused and more than a little nervous. She thought again of Miss Caroline's anxiety about this trip to Hawaii.

"Probably been watching our driveway."

"Will this be on the newscast?"

"Likely, it will be. The navy isn't handing out any information on the investigation. You know reporters—they've got to know everything that's going on."

As soon as they got home, Roselina called Linc, for she didn't want him to hear about the episode from someone else. When she hung up, Roselina said, "At least he isn't mad at me. He says there's nothing we can do about it. If he calls the TV station and tries to get them to forget about the incident, they'll think you know something and will keep pestering you."

Maddie was at the cottage when Linc came home, and he asked Roselina, "Did the television reporters distress her?"

"Not much. I was more upset than she was. Will it be on the evening news?"

"I hope not, but we'll watch and see."

Maddie was on her way to help Roselina when she met Linc coming from his dip in the ocean. He had a large beach towel wrapped around his shoulders, and his dampened hair clung to his shapely head.

"Are you okay?" he asked her, his eyes betraying his concern.

"Sure. It happened so fast, I didn't have time to get scared. Roselina moved in on the guy, warned him off and rushed me into the car. Are you going to say, 'I told you so'?"

"Of course not. We made the decision that you'd stay, so we'll deal with what comes along."

"I prayed about our decision, and I feel at peace with it. Everything will work out all right."

"I've been doing some praying myself," he said as they walked side by side into the house. "I haven't prayed for so long it's almost like a new experience. I hadn't had anyone to share my problems for years, and it's a great feeling to know that God is on my side."

"Yes, and when He is, we don't have to fear anything, but I want to watch the newscast tonight in case they air the incident. I must have made a spectacle of myself. I was so startled, I couldn't even talk. About all I could do was mumble."

Laughing, Linc said, "Perhaps that's just as well. You weren't required to answer his questions."

They ate dinner in the kitchen so they could watch the news on Roselina's television. The photographer hadn't missed any of the interview nor Roselina's rapid departure. When Maddie laughed at the startled-deer expression on her face, Roselina and Linc laughed, too.

"After seeing that distorted picture," Linc said, "no one would ever suspect it was you."

But still when bedtime came, and he walked with her to the guesthouse as he always did, he said, "Maddie, I'll feel more at ease if you move into the main house. This cottage isn't burglarproof. You think about it and we'll decide tomorrow." He went inside and checked the locks on the windows and doors.

"We're pretty safe here except from the ocean, and I'm sure you'll be all right tonight."

When he returned to the house, Roselina had already gone to her room, but he tapped on her door.

"Come in, Mr. Linc. I'm not in bed."

Roselina relaxed in a lounge chair in a voluminous robe, and she eyed her employer with a question in her deep-set, dark eyes. He shuffled from one foot to the other.

"I'm worried about Maddie being alone in the cottage. What do you think about shifting the bed from the spare room and preparing quarters for her in the enclosed gallery. Maddie will have a view of the ocean, and with the couch and chairs in that room, she'll have more privacy than if she only has the bedroom for her use."

He looked straight at Roselina, wondering what she thought, and he soon learned.

"And it will be more proper for her to be sleeping at the far end of the hall, close to my room, rather than in the bedroom right across the hall from you. That's the only solution—she shouldn't stay in that cottage alone. I'll help you move the bed."

They worked for an hour moving furniture and rearranging the big spacious room. Surveying their work, Roselina said, "This *is* a better arrangement. She can even see Honolulu on a clear day. I'll move my things out of the bathroom I've been using, so she can have a private bath."

"Oh, I don't expect you to do that," he protested.

"That's the best way. You and I can share a bathroom. Or I can use the one downstairs."

Linc put his arms around Roselina and hugged her tightly. "You're a prize, my friend. Don't ever leave me."

She patted his face. "I don't intend to until you find another lady to take over your household."

Giving him a pert glance, she left him alone in the room they'd prepared for Maddie.

Linc came to the guesthouse before breakfast to discuss the change in arrangements he and Roselina had made with Maddie. She liked the cottage, but she did feel isolated in it, so Maddie didn't argue about moving to the main house.

"Do you want me to move today?" she asked Linc. "It won't take long."

"Yes. Roselina will show you where to go. I think it's better this way."

Maddie did feel safer in her new bedroom. She was far enough away that she didn't hear Linc going and coming, but the soft stirring of Roselina as she moved in the room next door was comforting to her. Maddie had never lived alone, and she preferred living in the main house.

The next morning when Maddie went for her early-morning swim, she returned by way of the cottage. Her heart stopped when she saw a big hole in one of the glass doors. She peered inside and saw a lava rock in the middle of the floor. She started to open the door, but decided that wasn't a wise move.

She ran to the house and collided with Linc as she darted in the kitchen door. He caught her in his arms, disturbed by the expression on her face.

"What is it?"

She gasped for breath, and he held her away from him.

"The guesthouse," she stammered. "The glass door is shattered."

Roselina turned quickly from the sink where she was peeling oranges for their breakfast.

"God, help us," she whispered.

"You stay here," Linc said to Maddie. She shook her head and followed him out of the house. He held her hand as they hurried toward the cottage.

"Don't be upset," he tried to soothe her. "Sometimes a large seabird flies into windows and breaks them."

"It would have been a mighty big bird to have carried that rock," she said with a slight smile. By that time they'd reached the cottage, and Linc said, "You stay outside while I check everything out."

When she opened her mouth to protest, he squeezed her hand. "I mean it."

Trembling, she waited, watching him through the open door. After he checked the whole building, he knelt beside the large rock on the floor. He motioned for Maddie to come in.

"Don't touch anything," he said.

She crept close to him. The large chunk of lava had a newspaper tied around it. Using the tips of his fingers, Linc unwrapped a sheet of newspaper that was turned to the article about the Sanale brothers' escape from prison.

Maddie covered her face with her trembling hands and leaned against the kitchen bar.

"Let's go back to the house. I must notify the police, and I don't want to use this phone. We'll leave the cottage as we found it."

"Whoever did this apparently didn't know that I'd moved."

"I suppose so," he said grimly.

"Why would anybody be intimidating me because my father was killed here ten years ago?"

"People with sick minds will do anything." He lifted her hand and rubbed it along his face before he released it. "Don't worry. I'll protect you." As they walked to the house, he continued to hold her hand.

"It isn't right for me to involve you in my problems," she said slowly. "I should have gone home as you wanted me to."

"It's only two weeks before you're scheduled to leave, so we'll keep you safe until then."

"I can't bear to think of going home until I know what really happened to my father."

He couldn't think of her going home at all, but he said, "I'll call you often and keep you aware of what's happening. This investigation could continue for years."

The police spent most of the day checking out the grounds. Since Linc had gates to his property that automatically locked at midnight, the police were inclined to think that the attackers had come by sea.

After the other officers left, Claudia Warren and Linc went into his office.

"It would be an easy matter for them to come ashore, run up to the guesthouse and heave the rock inside," she indicated.

"At least Miss Horton isn't staying in the cottage now," Linc said.

"I have no doubt that the Sanale family is responsible for this. Kamu has gone underground, and I imagine that's where he'll stay. They have plenty of cousins to do their dirty work for them, but I doubt they'll do Miss Horton any harm. We'll have our water patrol keep watch on your cove for a while. We'll notify the naval base of what's happening."

Linc reluctantly returned to work the next day. He could hardly bear to have Maddie out of his sight, but he made both Roselina and Maddie promise that they wouldn't leave the property without telling him where they were going. When he left, he closed the gates.

In spite of this new threat to her peace of mind, as Christmas approached Maddie realized that she was happier than she'd been during any Christmas season since her mother had gotten sick. The years with Miss Caroline hadn't been too lonely because most of the others at VOH didn't have family members present, either. But the holiday had been a quiet affair, except for the Christmas Eve church service.

Last year at Christmas, a cousin of her mother's had invited Maddie for the holidays, and she'd gone, thinking it would be a break from the usual routine. It had been a miserable experience because the cousin's grandchildren were noisy and unruly. She was thankful that Linc's invitation had spared her a repeat visit with her relatives.

As she and Roselina shopped for the Christmas dinner and baked cookies to put in boxes for the elderly church members, she knew she was a help. She carried most of the groceries to the car and into the house—legwork that Roselina had done by herself in other years.

Linc closed his offices for a three-day holiday so his employees could be at home with family. He turned down several invitations from his business associates to spend Christmas Eve at their homes.

Since Linc would be home all day on the twenty-fourth, Maddie waited until then to trim the tree. Roselina had insisted that Maddie should buy exactly what she wanted. She had color coordinated the various-size ornaments in blue and rose. The electric lights were small seashells in a brownish-rose color. A blue-robed angel adorned the top of the tree. After they draped several ropes of silver tinsel around the tree, they stood back to admire their efforts. Maddie believed it was the most beautiful Christmas tree she'd ever seen. Roselina agreed with her.

Linc had had all of his gifts professionally wrapped. While Roselina and Maddie worked in the kitchen preparing dinner, he brought them from the garage. Even while he questioned the wisdom of it, Linc had bought many things for Maddie. Every time he saw something he thought she would like, he bought it and ended up with fifteen gifts for her. Roselina entered the room and lifted her eyebrows humorously when he spread all the gaily wrapped packages under the tree. Linc felt his face burning.

They ate their meal at four o'clock so they could finish in time for the Christmas Eve service held on Waikiki Beach.

When Linc went upstairs to dress for the evening, Roselina whispered, "Thank God, Mr. Linc is going with us. I've prayed for him for years. God heard my prayers and sent you to us, Miss Maddie. You've made a big change in his life."

Maddie blushed and wouldn't look at Roselina.

The interdenominational service was scheduled a half hour prior to the fall of darkness. Seated in a semicircle of padded chairs arranged to accommodate three hundred people, space usually used for a hotel's luau, the audience faced the ocean. As the choir sang anthems, and four ministers read the Christmas story from Matthew and Luke, the sky changed constantly. An outrigger canoe passed by with a band playing

Christmas carols. The sun dipped behind a cloud as the speaker brought the sermon to a close.

Maddie's heart was full of praise and worship, and tears of joy glistened in her eyes. She turned to Linc and their eyes met and held for an interminable moment. Maddie's blood scampered through her veins like a tidal wave, before her heartbeat slowly settled to its natural rhythm. Her physical reaction to Linc stunned her as if she'd been hit by a stroke of lightning.

Maddie knew without doubt that she loved Linc, not with the immaturity of a child, but with the full-blown emotion of a woman's heart. Before she turned away, she believed she detected a sense of wonder in his gray eyes, as if he, too, had realized he loved her. But whatever his feelings toward her, Maddie knew that she belonged to him forever.

The pageantry and beauty of the service had blessed all of them, and they drove back to the house almost in silence. When Linc unlocked the door, he said, "Should we open most of our gifts tonight? And perhaps save a few boxes for tomorrow when the Kingsburys are with us. I have gifts for them, so we'll keep some of our things to open when they're here."

"Suits me, Mr. Linc," Roselina said. "You know I'm just like a kid when it comes to opening gifts."

Maddie went to her room to take off the light-weight jacket she'd worn to the service. She was fidgety, wondering if Linc would like the gift she'd gotten for him, even though Roselina had assured her it was a suitable gift.

Since the police agreed with Linc that Maddie shouldn't go anyplace alone, Roselina and Maddie had shopped together for Linc's gifts.

"Mr. Linc usually receives a lot of expensive gifts from his business associates, but I always buy several little trinkets for him," Roselina had said while they shopped.

Maddie had agonized over what to buy Linc, until she finally decided to have an enlargement made of her photo that she carried in her billfold. The picture had been taken the year before for a university publication. But after she had the eight-by-ten photo made, matted and framed, Maddie wondered if she was being presumptuous to assume that Linc would want her picture. But she'd spent quite a lot on the gift and she couldn't afford anything else.

No doubt he would just accept the gift like a father receiving a picture from his daughter.

NINE

After her mother's death, Maddie hadn't received many gifts, and she shared Roselina's excitement about the presents under the tree. In spite of the suspense that had surrounded her since her arrival in Hawaii, as Christmas Eve settled around them, there were no shadows in Maddie's heart.

Roselina settled in a big armchair, and Maddie sat on the floor beside her while Linc distributed all of the packages. "I'll leave one box for each of us with the ones I have for Steve and Ahonui," he said. He'd deliberately left the black pearls and earrings set he'd bought for Maddie under the tree. It was his finest gift to her, and he wanted to save it for last.

"It's a custom in my family that the youngest opens gifts first and then we continue up the age level to the oldest," Roselina said. "So Miss Maddie, you go first."

"And we always opened our gifts on Christmas Eve when Mother and Daddy were alive," Maddie said. "So this seems like old times to have so many gifts under the tree."

Linc sorted Maddie's gifts and brought them to her one by one. He sat on the floor beside her as she opened them.

Briefly she wondered if she should accept so many gifts from Linc, but her joy in his gifts outweighed her pride. She tore into each box with the excitement of a four-year-old. She realized that Linc and Roselina were amused at her excitement. Only later would she wonder if Linc had bought the gifts because he thought of her as a daughter, or if there could be a deeper meaning.

Some of the gifts were more like toys—a hula girl figurine, and a grotesque carved wood male figure about a foot tall, which was called the Lucky or Aumakua Tiki. A shark's tooth necklace made of bone beads and hematite was the only other jewelry from him. He gave her a coconut purse, which was just the right size to strap around her waist and carry small essential items when they walked along the beach. There was another large Aloha handbag that matched the Summer Hibiscus pareo he'd purchased.

Picking up the pareo and feeling the soft fabric, Roselina said, "You can wrap this around your body in many ways. All Hawaiian women have them."

"I know. It's just what I need to wear back and forth to our beach."

Linc saved the largest box for the last, and Maddie was surprised into silence when she opened it to find a ukulele inside.

A tender expression in his eyes, Linc said,

"Since you sing so well, I thought you could learn to play the ukelele. There's a self-taught lesson book inside."

Maddie took the instrument from the leather case and strummed the strings.

"I can learn to play this easily," she said. "I have a guitar, which I often played when Janice and I sang together at VOH chapel service. Thank you so much for everything. I don't know how I'll ever get them home."

"I'll have them shipped for you," Linc said. Any problem she had, Linc was quick to solve it. But how would he solve her biggest problem—her love for him?

Opening Roselina's gifts of body lotions, stationery, a calendar and a muumuu was anticlimatic, but Maddie showed as much appreciation for them as she had for the gifts she'd received from Linc.

His gifts from his business associates included cheese and nut sets, shaving lotion, cufflinks, as well as gift boxes of Hawaiian products.

When he opened the portrait of Maddie, he was speechless. The photographer had captured all of her beauty—physical and spiritual—on the camera. For a moment, he forgot that Roselina was in the room.

"You couldn't have given me anything I'd like more," he said softly. "Did you have it made here?"

"The picture was taken at the beginning of last school year. I had the enlargement made in Honolulu."

"Thank you." The words sounded inadequate, but

what else could he say that wouldn't reveal the depth of his feelings for her?

"Maybe it will make you remember me after I leave Hawaii."

The thought of having Maddie leave his home was becoming more and more unpleasant. He hadn't known how empty the house had seemed before. He enjoyed his home, but he'd spent a lot of time away from it. Now that Maddie was in the house, he eagerly watched his office clock for five o'clock to come. Generally, she was watching for him and stepped out on the veranda and waved to him as he drove into the garage. Would he be foolish to let her return to her home without giving her the opportunity to stay with him?

Roselina had several gifts from her children and grandchildren in California, and from her sister, who lived in Honolulu. Linc had bought lengths of fabric for her as she liked to make her own clothes. He also gave her a check for a thousand dollars.

When the gifts were all opened, Roselina said, "Hey, one of you give me a hand. I've been sitting here so long, I can't get up. We've got to get this mess cleaned up before company comes tomorrow."

Linc took her hand to assist her out of the chair.

"There's no hurry. I told Ahonui we wouldn't eat until midafternoon. But we should put our things under the tree and dispose of the wrapping and ribbons."

"If you and Miss Maddie will do that, I'll make a few preparations in the kitchen. Everybody takes care of their own breakfast in the morning," she warned.

Maddie separated the gifts they were to open tomorrow from the ones they'd opened. She took the sweeper from the closet and cleaned the carpet while Linc disposed of the wrapping paper.

"Thank you again for all your gifts. It's been a wonderful evening."

"So you don't mind that I brought you so far away from home for Christmas?"

Mind! she thought wildly. She felt more at home now than she'd ever felt in her life. But to Linc, she said, "I wouldn't have wanted to spend Christmas anywhere else. It's the best Christmas I've had since I was a little girl, and I was with Mother and Daddy opening our gifts together. Can you remember your best Christmas, Linc?"

"That isn't hard to recall," he said with a slight tremor in his voice. "It's this one."

His gray eyes blazed with an emotion that Maddie wasn't sure she understood, but it filled her heart with a strange inner excitement. She turned away, wondering how to interpret the message his eyes flashed in her direction.

Maddie didn't go to sleep for a long time after she went to bed, thinking about all the gifts Linc had bought for her. He'd made it a point to convince her that he was interested in her because he had been her father's friend. So did he buy the presents for that reason or because he had another interest in her?

What was his problem? Did he think he was too

old for her? Or didn't she appeal to him in a romantic sense?

She didn't think of Linc as her father's friend. There wasn't any doubt in her mind that the childish infatuation she'd carried for ten years had become something much more important. She knew she shouldn't read more into his gift giving than he'd intended. Still, since it was Christmas Eve, she indulged herself and lay awake wondering about the message his eyes had conveyed—thinking how wonderful it would be if Linc was in love with her.

Maddie awakened when she heard Roselina leave her room. She wanted to do her share of the work and hurried out of bed and into the bathroom to prepare for the day. Dressed in capris and a knit shirt, she arrived in the kitchen at seven o'clock.

Roselina was working at the sink peeling and deveining the shrimp they'd gotten at the market yesterday. She wore a brightly colored muumuu, which had been one of Linc's gifts. She hummed "Silent Night" softly. Roselina didn't know Maddie was in the kitchen until she said, "Merry Christmas! What can I do to help?"

Roselina glanced over her shoulder and scolded, "What are you doing up so early?"

"I want to help. Just tell me what to do."

"You can set and decorate the table, but fix yourself some breakfast first."

Linc wandered into the kitchen wearing the long

robe Roselina had given him. He looked sleepy, and his hair was disheveled.

"How can a guy sleep when the two of you are bustling around the house?"

"I suppose you came to help, too?" Roselina said, a gleam in her eye.

"No such thing. I won't help until I've had my breakfast."

"Which you'll have to fix yourself," she retorted. "I told you I'd be busy today."

"What do you want for breakfast?" Maddie asked. "I'm going to fix toast, Hawaiian style, for myself. Would you like a serving of that?"

"I would. While you do that, I'll prepare a pot of coffee, since my housekeeper refuses to help."

Maddie cut two thick slices of bread from the loaves Roselina had baked the day before. She put slices of ham, pineapple and Gouda cheese on each piece of bread and arranged them on a cooking sheet. She turned the oven temperature on low heat and baked the toast until the cheese melted. She garnished the toast with a few ripe cherries. It gave her a warm feeling to be preparing Linc's food.

By one o'clock, the buffet was ready, and the three of them went to their bedrooms to change. Maddie wore the Hawaiian dress—a white fabric with red poinsettias sprinkled lavishly across it—that Roselina had bought for her. Roselina changed into another muumuu, and Linc wore a green turtleneck and white trousers.

As usual, Ahonui and Steve came earlier than expected. As Maddie went out on the veranda with Linc to greet the guests, the sun shone brightly, the temperature was in the seventies and a pleasant breeze wafted from the ocean. She couldn't believe it was Christmas Day.

Steve carried three gifts, which he handed to Maddie. "You can put these under the tree."

"Merry Christmas, Linc," Ahonui said. "And you, too, Maddie."

"Thanks—the same to you."

Ahonui seemed friendly enough, but Maddie was still uncomfortable around her. She felt mean-spirited to be jealous of his secretary, when she was sure that Linc hadn't spent any time with Ahonui, except in the office, since she had arrived in Hawaii.

Maddie carried the boxes and put them under the tree.

"We opened our gifts last night," Linc said, "but we kept one each to open when you came. Roselina and Maddie have dinner prepared, but we might as well open our gifts now."

"Opening gifts on Christmas Eve?" Steve said, lifting his heavy eyebrows.

"It's customary in Maddie's and Roselina's families, and I liked it," Linc said tersely.

Maddie's gift from the Kingsburys was a set of Hawaiian lotions and perfumes, which she did appreciate. Roselina was given a tote bag containing several romance books, puzzle books and a white shawl. The Kingsburys had gotten Linc a silver ring inset with a large ruby.

Ahonui exclaimed over the long, golden chain Linc gave her. "I'll give you the privilege of putting it around my neck for the first time."

Maddie busied herself with opening a bottle of perfume and sniffing it when Ahonui backed up to Linc and held the necklace out to him.

"So I get the largest gift," Steve said as he tore the wrappings from a bag for his golf clubs.

"Just what I needed," he said. "The guys I play with have been warning me to buy a new golf bag before I lose all of my clubs."

The last gift to be opened was the small box Linc had withheld from Maddie the night before. "I hope you'll enjoy wearing these," he said softly, his voice as intimate as if they were alone.

Her eyes widened, and she looked up at Linc in amazement, when she removed the wrappings of the box containing a choker necklace set with a seven-cluster of Tahitian black pearls. A set of matching pearl earrings was in the box.

"Oh, Linc," she said breathlessly. Quickly, she took off the necklace and earrings she wore. Handing the necklace to him, she said, "Help me, will you?"

His hands trembled until he could hardly fasten the pearls around her neck. Maddie didn't seem aware of his shortness of breath as she busily inserted the black pearls in her ears.

Excited, she left her chair and went to the mirror

over the chest beside the stairway. The jewelry didn't do anything for the dress she wore, but she intended to wear them the rest of the day. Linc must have known that the silver-hued pearls would contrast vividly with her ivory skin. She lifted her eyes to the mirror and held Linc's clear gray ones as he watched her pleasure in his gift. A tense, exciting silence filled the room until Ahonui broke the spell.

"That's a very nice gift," she said.

"I'll say!" Maddie answered excitedly. "I've admired them in the shop windows, but I never expected to own any. Thanks, Linc. You're spoiling me."

"My pleasure," he said, dismissing her thanks with a wave of his hand.

They ate leisurely, and the Kingsburys lingered until late evening. Ahonui insisted that they must watch a special sailing event around Oahu featured on late-night television. Roselina wanted to telephone her children, and she excused herself and went to her room soon after dinner. Maddie watched the sailboats for a while, but when she kept yawning, she curled up in a corner of the big couch and went to sleep.

When they finally left at midnight, Ahonui said, "I'm sorry we bored your houseguest with the sailing."

"I doubt she was bored," Linc said with a fond look at Maddie, who lay on her side, her hand under her right cheek. "She's tired. We were up late last night, and she got up early this morning to help prepare dinner. Don't wake her."

He waved the Kingsburys on their way, locked the door and returned to the living room. Stopping by the couch, he looked down at Maddie. What was he going to do about her?

"Maddie," he said, and when she continued to sleep, he touched her shoulder and shook her gently. She sighed deeply and turned on her back. He decided to leave her where she was, and went to the closet under the stairway and brought a blanket. When he spread it over her, Maddie opened her eyes and stretched. She rubbed her eyes and looked around the empty room.

"Have Ahonui and Steve gone? That wasn't polite of me to go to sleep. I'm sorry."

"No need to be. I'm sleepy, too." He took her hand to lift her off the couch. She caught her feet in the blanket and stumbled against him. His arms closed around her waist.

"Sorry I'm so clumsy," she said, kicking her feet free of the blanket. When his hold tightened around her waist, Maddie lifted her eyes to his. Throwing caution to the wind, he kissed her.

"I hope you didn't mind," he whispered.

She shook her head, and the fine strands of her hair swirled over his shoulders. "I didn't mind at all," she answered softly. "It made my Christmas complete."

He kissed her again and this time she responded with intensity. Linc quickly scanned his future—a future he couldn't envision without Maddie. Why was he reluctant to tell her he loved her? Would he be taking advantage of her to ask her to marry him at his age? And if she said yes, would he always wonder if she'd married him out of gratitude? Still, he reasoned, the way she responded to his caresses was more than gratitude.

Linc told himself that he was acting like a love-struck teenage boy when he didn't want to go to work after the Christmas break. He had ten days with Maddie before she went home, and he had to force himself to leave her. Should he tell her how he felt about her and ask her to stay? But in a few weeks time, it was too soon to expect Maddie to make a decision about marrying him. When she had no family to advise her, would he be taking advantage of her youth if he proposed to her?

Since he had no justifiable excuse, he went to the office the day after Christmas and immersed himself in some work that had to be completed before the first of the year. He had turned off his computer and was locking his desk ready to go home to Maddie when the phone rang. He was ready to leave his office, when Ahonui spoke over the intercom.

"There's a man on the line. He won't give a name, but he says he has an urgent message for you."

"All right," Linc said impatiently. He walked back to his desk and pushed the talk button on his phone.

A guttural voice said, "Don't think she can hide behind you. If we need to, we'll remove *you,* then take our quarry."

The caller hung up, and Linc slumped against the desk, still holding the phone in his hand, too stunned to move. The voice had seemed disguised to him. He wasn't sure whether the caller was a man or a woman.

Ahonui came in immediately and looked at him— a strange, excited light in her eyes. He tried to compose his features, wondering if she'd listened in on the call. He didn't want this warning to be circulated around the office.

"Is everything all right?" she asked.

"Yes. Is there anything else needing my attention before I go home?"

"No. I've been wanting to take Maddie to lunch or dinner before she leaves Hawaii. How much longer will she be here?"

"Her return flight is scheduled for the fourth of January. I have several things planned for her, but I'll tell her about your invitation."

With this further threat against Maddie, he'd have to guard her more closely. He wasn't sure that Ahonui would be able to protect her. Maybe he should just stay away from the office and watch her.

He sensed Ahonui's eyes boring into his back as he left the office, and he wondered if she'd listened to the phone call.

In the car, Linc used his cell phone to call Detective Warren. When he told her about the call, she said, "I'll try to trace it, but chances are, it came from a pay phone. There's little hope of finding the caller if that's the case, but we're keeping our eyes on the Sanale family living in Honolulu. I'll be in touch."

Although Linc usually obeyed the traffic laws to the letter, his foot pressed heavier and heavier on the accelerator the nearer he came to home. He considered himself a sensible man, so why did he keep having these horrible images of Maddie in danger? Had she been kidnapped already? Short of sending her home, which he couldn't bear to think of, what could he do to keep her safe? He was driving twenty miles over the speed limit when he reached the driveway to his house. He turned off the highway so quickly that the car tilted and almost overturned.

Shaking his head, he slowed to a reasonable speed. He didn't bother to put the car in the garage when he reached the house but stopped in front of the veranda. He switched off the engine and jumped out of the car in one swift movement. The front door stood open and he hit the floor of the living room in a run.

"Maddie! Where are you?" he called as he ran through the downstairs.

Bounding up the stairs, he called, "Roselina, Maddie. Where are you?"

Roselina wouldn't go away and leave the house open unless it was an emergency. He stepped into Maddie's room and surveyed the beach front. A blanket was spread out on the sand, but he couldn't see Maddie. Had she been sunbathing and someone had taken her?

He ran from the house, but his heart was pounding in his chest. Gasping for breath, he slowed his steps to a brisk walk toward the beach. She wasn't on the blanket. He reached in his pocket for his cell phone to call the police when he heard Roselina's voice.

"What are you doing home so early, Mr. Linc? We hoped to surprise you."

He turned and went limp with relief. A table and grill had been set up in a small grove of palm trees that had blocked his view. Roselina walked from the guesthouse with a tray of meat and cooking utensils. Maddie was behind her carrying hamburger buns.

The two women stared at him in alarm, and he realized his appearance must be frightening. Maddie rushed to his side. "What's wrong?"

He hugged her in a tight embrace that lifted her feet from the ground.

"Thank God," he said, and he felt tears running down his face. His arms tightened. Only when he held her in his arms was he convinced she was safe!

Pounding him on the back, Roselina said, "Put her down, Mr. Linc. You're squashing her, as well as the hamburger buns."

"Sorry," he said, releasing Maddie. She tossed the mashed rolls toward the table and took hold of his hand. She sat beside him when he slumped down on the sand.

"What has happened?" Maddie insisted as she wiped the tears from his face with a napkin.

"I received a threatening phone call about you just as I was leaving work. I rushed home, and when I couldn't find either of you, and the house was open, I thought you'd been taken."

"What kind of message?"

"Something to the effect that I couldn't hide you all the time." His hands were shaking, and he bowed his head on his flexed knees. Maddie rubbed his bent shoulders.

"I'm all right, so try to forget it."

He shook his head. "I can't forget it. We're dealing with a predator who has a warped mind. I don't know how to keep you safe."

Maddie was more concerned about Linc than her own safety at the moment. "I should have gone home when you asked me to."

He shook his head. "I would worry even more, not to be able to check on you. I have work that has to be completed before the end of the year which will take a couple of days for me to finish. After that, I'll stay home to look after you. I'm so upset now I can't think what to do, but I'll come up with something."

"'God is our refuge and strength, a very present help in time of trouble,'" Maddie quoted one of her favorite Scripture passages. "God will look after me."

TEN

Linc forced himself to go to work the next day, after warning Roselina to be on guard, and to keep the doors locked.

"I'll watch over her the best I can, Mr. Linc. You'll have to get hold of yourself."

Linc hadn't forgotten his training with firearms in the navy. On his way to work, he stopped at the police station and got permission to carry a gun.

Maddie felt like a prisoner because Linc had told her not to leave the house, but she didn't want to cause him any concern. She settled down in his office and tried to organize the materials she found in the library.

The phone rang around midmorning. When Maddie saw on the Caller ID that it was the corporate offices of Carey Enterprises, she answered.

After a brief greeting, Ahonui said, "Linc received a threatening phone call yesterday."

"I know. He told me about it."

Ahonui didn't respond for several seconds. "Oh,

he did! And you're still in his house! Aren't you concerned about his safety?"

"Linc's safety! I thought I was the one who was threatened. He didn't say anything about a threat to him."

"Naturally, he wouldn't, and I don't want you to tell anyone that I warned you, or I'll be in danger, too. The caller threatened Linc's life if he continues to harbor you. For your own good, as well as Linc's, you should go home."

Maddie's mouth was so dry she couldn't speak, and she hung up without answering. She didn't want to risk Linc's life. What should she do? What *could* she do?

She wondered briefly if this was something Ahonui had trumped up just to get rid of her. Maddie could hardly believe that Ahonui could be jealous of *her*, but Linc had been very attentive to Maddie when the Kingsburys had visited on Christmas Day. But she had to admit that she had never detected anything more than friendship between them.

Roselina had been sweeping the veranda, and she hadn't heard the phone, so Maddie didn't have to explain about the caller. If Linc was threatened, Roselina could also be harmed for helping her so she was on her own in this decision.

Linc didn't come home for the evening meal, for he had to attend a Chamber of Commerce dinner. After Roselina and Maddie shared a quiet dinner, Maddie went to her room to pray and seek God's guidance. Even if she didn't want to go home, she couldn't live in Linc's house any longer. That posed a problem, for she didn't have enough money to stay any length of time in a hotel. And would it even be safe for her to be alone?

But as she prayed, Maddie realized that she was never alone, for God was with her. She asked for some tangible assurance that He was watching over her. She picked up her Bible and it fell open at the thirty-second Psalm. She scanned the verses, accepting the message God had for her.

The Psalmist had acknowledged,

You are my hiding place; You will protect me from trouble and surround me with songs of deliverance.

And God had answered,

I will instruct you and teach you in the way you should go; I will counsel you and watch over you.

Maddie didn't doubt that this was God's promise to her at this time. *But, God, which way should I go?*

While she waited for God's answer, Maddie remembered the example of Gideon in the Old Testament.

God had called Gideon to command an attack on the enemies of the Israelites. Because his family was insignificant, Gideon couldn't believe that God had asked him to undertake a task that he believed was doomed for failure. When God persisted, Gideon assembled an army, but he still wondered if he'd misinterpreted God's message.

Maddie opened her Bible to the book of Judges and read Gideon's words to God.

If You will save Israel by my hand as You have promised—look, I will place a wool fleece on the threshing floor. If there is dew only on the fleece and all the ground is dry, then I will know that You will save Israel by my hand as You said.

The next morning, Gideon squeezed a bowlful of water out of the fleece. Still unsatisfied, Gideon put God to the test again. He laid the fleece out once more and asked God for one further assurance. The second night Gideon prayed that the fleece would be dry and the grass wet. When this happened, Gideon knew that God had indeed spoken to him, and he led his army to victory over the enemies of the Israelites.

God, my request is simple—please put the answer in my mind while I sleep so I'll know what to do when I wake up in the morning.

Maddie turned off the light and snuggled beneath the soft blanket believing that the next day she'd have the answer. She hadn't gone to sleep when Linc came home, and when he tapped lightly on her door, she answered and assured him that she was all right.

* * *

Of course, Maddie thought even before she opened her eyes the next morning. *Stella Oliver, Miss Caroline's friend.* Before she'd started to Hawaii, she had promised Miss Caroline that she would visit her friend, but in all the excitement of Christmas, the promise had slipped her mind.

Stella Oliver, who operated a facility much like VOH in Honolulu, would be able to advise her on what to do. Since God had provided the answer, Maddie believed He would also guide her in getting in touch with Mrs. Oliver.

Roselina had some medical tests to take that day, and she was concerned that she shouldn't leave Maddie alone. She insisted that Maddie should go with her, but when Linc was consulted, he thought that Maddie would be safer at his home with all the doors and windows locked.

"I'll be all right," Maddie assured her when Roselina was ready to leave. "I have plenty of things to do. Lock all of the doors, and I'll be all right."

Maddie had already looked up the telephone number of Open Arms Shelter, the facility where Stella Oliver worked. When Roselina's car was out of sight, she called Stella.

As soon as she identified herself, Stella said, "Oh, yes. In her Christmas letter, Caroline indicated that you'd be calling. When are you coming by to see me?"

Roselina didn't expect to return until late afternoon, and Maddie believed she could visit Stella and be home without Roselina or Linc knowing about it. She hated to deceive these two people who had been so kind to her, but she was doing it for their own safety.

When she asked for directions, Stella said, "I'll send our van after you. We're located in a dangerous section of town, and I don't want you riding the bus or in a taxi."

As best she could, Maddie explained how to reach Linc's home, and within an hour the van from Open Arms Shelter arrived at the door. She took the spare key from Linc's office and locked the door behind her. The bus driver was a taciturn man, which suited Maddie's mood. During the hour's drive she fretted about how angry and worried Linc would be if he came home and found her gone.

The location of Open Arms Shelter in no way compared to the Valley of Hope, which was located in an alpine valley. VOH consisted of twenty or more brick buildings situated among well-kept lawns. Open Arms Shelter was in a four-story brick building surrounded by decrepit warehouses, many of them vacant. Maddie saw several apartment houses on the street. The shelter fronted on the sidewalk. Although appalled at the surroundings, Maddie conceded that the inhabitants of this section of town certainly needed a place of refuge.

She was admitted through a bolted door into a narrow hallway, where Stella was on hand to meet her. She invited Maddie to her office on the second floor.

Stella Oliver looked nothing like Miss Caroline, but Maddie felt the same confidence in Stella's presence that Miss Caroline had always instilled in her.

Stella was probably ten years younger than Miss Caroline. Her hair was dark brown with only a few wisps of gray, while Miss Caroline's was totally white. Caroline was a small woman. Stella was tall and angular. The problems of their residents seemed to have left an indelible path on each of their wrinkled faces. Stella's eyes were dark brown and Miss Caroline's were a brilliant blue, but each woman's eyes expressed the compassion and love in her heart.

"And how do you like our state?" Stella asked when she assured herself that Maddie was comfortably seated.

"Very well, until the past few days. I hesitate to bother you with my troubles, but I do need some guidance. I can only stay a short time, so I'll get to the point right away. Since you know Miss Caroline, I thought I could come to you."

"Of course you can. Caroline speaks highly of you, and I know she'd want me to help you. But I can't imagine why you would be having trouble in Hawaii."

"Did you see the notice in the paper a few weeks ago about the investigation into the death of Stanley Horton ten years ago?"

"I believe I heard something about it on television or radio." Stella peered closely at Maddie, her eyes questioning.

"Stanley Horton was my father. Lincoln Carey, a close friend of my father, is the one who invited me to visit him in Hawaii."

"Yes, Caroline mentioned that."

Continuing with the escape of the two men involved in the possible murder of her father until Linc's threatening telephone call, Maddie told Stella about the frightening incidents she had encountered.

"It's troubling me that I'm putting Linc in danger by staying at his house, but it will be useless for me to go back home until I know the outcome of the investigation of Daddy's death. With all of this on my mind, I wouldn't be able to concentrate on my studies at all."

"I can see why this would be a problem to you," Stella agreed. "What can I do to help?"

"Let me take refuge at Open Arms Shelter for a few weeks. I'll be willing to work to pay for my keep."

"We can always use volunteer work, so that wouldn't be a problem, and you're welcome to stay here. But I wonder if this area is safe for you, either."

"Not even if I stayed inside all the time."

"This is a rough neighborhood, and the man who's threatening you might be hiding in this area," Stella said. "Open Arms Shelter was organized for abused children and teenage girls. It's sort of like a halfway house. They stay here until the welfare representatives can find homes for them, so we have different people in and out almost every day. It will be easy for them to innocently mention you, and your enemies would soon learn where you're living. However, you're welcome to come, but shouldn't Mr. Carey know where you are?"

"I could leave him a note and tell him why I left. For his own safety, he shouldn't know where I am."

"It might work. But we would have to change your appearance. Your blond features would stand out vividly in this area. If you wear a wig and use a different name, you might be safe. What is your full name?"

"Madison Lee Horton."

"Hmm," Stella said thoughtfully. "Why not use Madison Lee? That way we wouldn't be telling a falsehood. A friend of mine operates a beauty shop— I think she'll provide a brunette wig for me."

"Then I must hurry back to Linc's home before he or Roselina come home. Roselina goes shopping tomorrow afternoon. If you don't hear anything from me, could you have your driver pick me up at two o'clock?"

Once these arrangements were made, Maddie was on pins and needles during the drive home. But she was fortunate to get back to the house before Roselina did.

She supposed it was due to a guilty conscience, but all through dinner, she thought Linc eyed her questioningly. When Roselina refused her help with clearing away the supper things, Linc asked, "What would you like to do? You've been cooped up all day."

Maddie felt her face flushing because she was unaccustomed to deceit, and without meeting his eyes, she said, "Let's go to the beach. It would be restful to sit and look at the water."

Knowing this might be the last time she could be alone with Linc, she wanted to take advantage of the remaining hours.

"Good idea," he agreed. "I'd appreciate a little rest, too," he said as they walked to the beach. He carried two lounge chairs and followed behind her on the stepping stones. Her body swayed gracefully as she walked, reminding him of a waving palm tree.

Maddie sighed wistfully when she stretched out on the chair he unfolded for her. She seemed distant tonight, unlike her usual affectionate nature. As he sat beside her, Linc concluded that it was small wonder that she seemed distracted. Her life was being threatened. And he understood how that felt. Now that he had been warned, he was uneasy when he was in a place he couldn't guard his back.

When the silence seemed too long, he said, "Maddie, we haven't talked about your future. Do you need any help with your college expenses?"

More fatherly instincts, she thought wryly. "No. Mother put Daddy's insurance money in a trust fund for me to use for college expenses. It earned interest for eight years before I started to use it, and it will last until I've graduated and have a job."

"With all the things that have been going on, I haven't shown you all the places I'd intended to. I've almost finished the end-of-the-year work, and I'll spend next week taking you where you want to go. I don't want you to be a prisoner, and we'll be careful. Do you need any more research on World War II?"

"As I told you after we visited the USS *Arizona,* I'm not sure I can write a paper on that subject now. Since I've been confined to the house, I've been organizing the material I got at the library, and I have enough to prepare the paper. Right now, college is the furthest thing from my mind."

"Then you wasted your time making this visit?" he said, and one of his eyebrows lifted teasingly.

Daringly, with a slow, direct look, she said pointedly, "You know better than that."

Since she might not see him again after tomorrow, she couldn't leave without giving him some hint of how she felt about him.

His expression grew serious, and he reached out his hand. She placed hers in it. "I know," he admitted. "You said you can't think about school now. I understand that, for with all that is happening now, there are some things we can't talk about." His gray eyes held hers intently. "Do you understand what I'm saying?"

She sighed deeply. She knew he was right, but it would have made her leave-taking more bearable if he would say the words she longed to hear.

But he didn't speak, and they sat mostly in silence, holding hands for the rest of the evening. She kept thinking that tomorrow she'd be gone, and that Linc would be disappointed in her. Surely he would understand that she was doing it for him.

When darkness stole upon them from the Pacific, they stood and Maddie tried to store up the atmosphere of the area, so she'd never forget the time she'd spent here. Still without speaking, Linc gathered her snugly into his arms. She relaxed against him, having no desire to leave his embrace. She would have this moment to remember.

When they separated in the hallway in front of Linc's room, without touching her, he leaned forward and kissed her lips softly. Tears blinded Maddie as she hurried to her room. She didn't turn to look, but she felt that he was watching her, wondering at her mood.

She worked until past midnight on the note she would leave for him. Somehow she must make him understand why she had left his home.

Dear Linc:
Please forgive me for going away, but I'm doing it for you. Since your life has been threatened, I would never forgive myself if anything happened to you. After you've been so good to me, it isn't fair to cause you any danger. I'm canceling my flight back home. I have to stay in Hawaii until I know the outcome of this investigation. Maybe when this is over, we can be together again. Please don't try to find me. I will be safe. Read the first seven verses of Psalm thirty-seven. I've claimed that promise.
Maddie.

To Roselina, she wrote,

I'm going away to a safe place, so please don't worry about me. Pray for me. I'll miss both of you.

She got into bed, but sleep wouldn't come. A question kept rolling over and over in her mind.

When morning came, would she have the courage to leave Linc?

ELEVEN

Roselina's habits were as regular as the tides, and she left for shopping promptly at one o'clock. Maddie had an hour before the van came. On trembling legs, she walked into Linc's bedroom, where she hadn't been before, and propped the note on his dresser.

The faint scent of the musk cologne he preferred permeated the room. Feeling almost like a Peeping Tom, Maddie glanced around his bedroom. It was neat and well-ordered, just like Linc's life. Her heart almost stopped when she saw her portrait on the nightstand beside his bed. If she'd needed any proof that he had more than a daughterlike interest in her, wouldn't this be a good sign?

Wanting some tangible evidence of his presence to take with her, she opened the jewelry box on his dresser. She had the photo taken on Waikiki beach, but she needed something she could have with her all the time. She looked at the rings in his box, and feeling like a thief, with trembling hands, she took one that had a small diamond in a silver setting. He'd seldom worn it, so it must not be one of his favorites.

She picked up the note she'd written to him, intending to add a sentence that she'd taken the ring. She paused, fingering the opal ring she wore. She removed it from her hand, kissed the ring, and inserted it in the slot where the silver-diamond ring had been. Linc knew the opal ring was her most-prized possession. Perhaps her mother's ring would convince him how much she loved him.

She took Roselina's note to the kitchen and left it lying on the table, where she would see it as soon as she entered the kitchen. As she went to various markets, Roselina's weekly shopping took several hours. Maddie should be safely away before she found the note.

She went to her room, carried her luggage downstairs and waited by the front door for the van from Open Arms Shelter. Tears blurred her eyes as they drove away from the place that had meant so much to her.

Linc was negotiating with a salesman about furnishings for the new Everyday Luau when Roselina called.

"Mr. Linc," she shouted, and the panic in her voice raised the hair on the back of his neck. "Mr. Linc, come home. Miss Maddie is gone."

"You mean she's been kidnapped?"

"I don't think so. She left a goodbye note."

He slammed down the phone and grabbed his coat off the back of his chair.

"I'm sorry to leave," he said to the salesman, "but there's an emergency at home. Call in a few days for another appointment."

He buzzed Ahonui's office. "I'm leaving. I'll check in tomorrow." He severed the connection before she could question him.

Again, he broke every traffic law on record as he raced for home in his car. His thoughts were so erratic it was an effort to focus on handling an automobile. If she had gone away on her own, why had she done it? He should have been more watchful.

Roselina stood on the veranda, wringing her hands, tears running down her face. "It's my fault. I shouldn't have left her alone, but I didn't think anything would happen."

Linc took time to hug her. "You have to buy groceries—you couldn't watch her twenty-four hours a day. Have you learned anything else?"

"Her clothes are all gone, and there's a note on your dresser."

Linc took the steps two at a time. He'd hardly drawn a deep breath since he'd had Roselina's call, and he felt light-headed when he rushed into his room. He used his car key to open the envelope and sank heavily on the bed as he read her message.

"Oh, Maddie, why did you do this?" he whispered, and his mind whirled as he considered all the things that could be happening to her. She knew no one in Honolulu except Steve and Ahonui, and she didn't seem to like either of them much. Where could she have gone?

Roselina crept to the door. "Did she tell you where she was going?" He handed her the note. His throat was too tight to talk.

She gasped when she read his note. "How did she know that someone had threatened your life? I didn't know it. When did this happen?"

"That man who called a few days ago intimated that they'd kill me if they had to, to get to Maddie. I didn't tell anyone about it. I suppose either the switchboard operator or Ahonui could have listened to the message."

He went to his Caller ID and flipped through the messages of the past few days, hoping he could learn if anyone had called Maddie. He paused when he found a call from Carey Enterprises three days previously at twelve-thirty. He couldn't remember that he'd called home then.

"Sit down, Roselina," he said, for she was still hovering at the door, looking as if she would faint any minute. "Do you remember if I called home Wednesday afternoon?"

"I don't remember, Mr. Linc. Sometimes I asked Maddie to answer the phone."

"I haven't talked to her on the phone since she came here. Have you talked to Ahonui this week? Or anyone else from my office?"

She shook her head.

"Then I'd better have a talk with my office staff."

Feeling nauseated, Linc dialed the office and asked for Ahonui.

"I'm checking on calls to the house," he said, when she answered in the sugary tones she always used to customers. "Did you call here Wednesday?"

"What time?"

"Any time."

"Goodness, how do you expect me to remember? I handle hundreds of calls in a week's time."

"Let me be more specific. Did you talk to Maddie on the phone this week? And what did you say to her?"

She didn't answer, and he said angrily, "Maybe I'd better get at this another way, and you be careful, *very careful,* how you answer. Did you overhear a telephone call I received on Monday about quitting time?"

"Yes."

"Now answer the other question. Did you call Maddie about it?"

"Yes, I did," Ahonui said, anger also in her voice. "You're stupid to jeopardize your life to protect her. I thought she needed to know that her presence was dangerous for you. I thought she'd have sense enough to go home, but I suppose she's tattled to you."

"She didn't tell me about it. Maddie left, and I don't think she's gone back to the mainland. And you'd better hope I find her real soon or you can clean out your desk and leave."

Her angry shriek nearly deafened him. "You can't

mean that—after all I've done for you. You haven't been the same since she came here."

Knowing he was wasting time talking to Ahonui, Linc hung up. Roselina was crying softly.

"Why would she tell Maddie?"

"I can't imagine, but somehow I sense that it isn't because she was worried about me."

"Maybe she didn't want to lose her job if you were killed."

"She's an efficient worker—she would have no trouble finding another job. But I'll deal with her after I find Maddie."

"What can you do?"

"I'm going to pray before I do anything. And you pray, too. Maddie doesn't want to be found, and if she's in a safe place, that's okay. But for my own peace of mind, I *have* to know where she is."

Since his spiritual awakening at Hōnaunau, Linc had been praying nightly and reading his Bible, but his mind was numb now. He didn't know if he could pray.

"I'm going for a swim at the beach."

Roselina left the room. He took off his clothes and changed into his trunks and wrapped a short terry cloth robe around his body. When he opened his jewelry box to put away his ring and watch, Maddie's opal ring struck his vision like a spotlight. He snatched the ring out of its velvet setting, and realized that his silver and diamond ring was gone. What did this mean? Maddie had told him that she'd worn her mother's ring every day since her mother's death. Why had she left it behind? He read her note again to see if she'd mentioned the ring exchange, but he found nothing.

He reached for his Bible and read the verses Maddie had mentioned. Several times he read aloud, "'You are my hiding place; You will protect me from trouble and surround me with songs of deliverance.'"

The words comforted him somewhat, but as he walked toward the beach, the view that usually brought peace of mind was only a sad place today. He could see Maddie as he'd often watched her from the house as she played in the water or rested on the sand. He sat on a large rock and stared out across the water.

God, I know she has You to protect her, but for my own peace of mind I have to know where she is. Please help me make the right decision in looking for her, for I don't want her enemies to find her.

He swam for several minutes, then spread out on the sand to think. His decision made, he went back to the house and telephoned a private detective agency he'd used a few times. He asked for Ed Blake, a taciturn individual who hailed from Utah.

After he identified himself, Linc said, "I have a job I'd like for you to get on right away." He explained the situation.

"I'll come out to your house and look around if you don't mind," the detective said. "I'll be there in an hour."

Ed Blake was a nondescript man that most people

would never notice—an asset that contributed to his success as a detective. When Linc showed him Maddie's picture, he whistled and his usually sober eyes gleamed.

"It shouldn't be difficult to find her. She's a looker! I can see why you'd be concerned, though."

"You must be subtle in your investigation. I want to know where she is, but I don't want anyone else to know. If you can locate her in less than forty-eight hours, there will be a five-hundred-dollar bonus for you."

"You've said that you can account for all of your phone calls, but with your permission, I'll find out what calls she might have made from your house phone or the phone in the cottage."

Linc wrote a memo and signed it to expedite the detective's search at the phone company.

"Does she have any friends in Honolulu?"

"She's met a few people at my office and in the church, but no one that she has more than a speaking acquaintance with."

Suddenly he stopped and slapped his forehead with the palm of his hand. "She did mention a few days ago about visiting a woman in Honolulu who's a friend of someone she knows at home. This friend lives in West Virginia, and she can tell me who Maddie might be visiting here in Hawaii. But I'm not sure how to contact this woman, so I'll give you a few days to find out what you can. I don't want to worry Maddie's friends back home unless I have to."

* * *

After living in Linc's comfortable home for almost a month, Maddie felt as if she was back in her university dormitory room when she moved her belongings into the austere room Stella Oliver provided for her. Open Arms Shelter was established in an old hotel which had been a plush establishment until hard times hit the neighborhood.

Motioning to one side of the room that showed signs of occupancy, Stella said, "You'll be sharing a room with Ailina Zadok, one of our teachers. While you settle in, I'll see about getting a wig for you. I'll look for a pair of glasses with tinted plain glass in them, which will also change your appearance. If you have some Hawaiian clothes, wear them."

"I have a few native garments."

"I wish I had a private room for you, but there aren't any. Rooming with someone else, you won't be able to conceal your identity. However, Ailina is about your age. She will keep your confidence."

"I appreciate what you're doing for me. I hope I'm not putting *you* in any danger. In my concern for Linc's safety, I didn't think of that."

"We're often threatened by the families of those we try to help, so I'm used to that. But our mission group named this place Open Arms Shelter to reach out a helping hand to anyone who needs it. You need help, and you're welcome here."

"Thanks. You remind me of Miss Caroline."

"Which I consider a great compliment. Caroline gave up a lot to establish the Valley of Hope."

"What should I call you?" Maddie asked. "The children at VOH applied Miss to Caroline, and the residents call her Miss Caroline now."

"I'm Stella to most everyone, although some of the children call me Māmā. I accept that, for most of them need a mother's influence in their lives. Just call me Stella."

Maddie couldn't believe the difference the wig and glasses made in her appearance. The wig was dark brown and the glasses were faintly tinted until her eyes were a nondescript color. She put on one of the muumuus that Roselina had bought for her, applied a dark makeup base, and she hardly recognized herself.

"Where did I go?" she said to Stella when she went to her office to model the results. Stella laughed, saying, "You're still beautiful, but at least your clothes and the other regalia hide your most obvious Caucasian features."

"So what am I going to do to earn my keep?"

"You can work here in my office each morning. You're probably better on a computer than I am, and you can catch up with reports that are overdue to our mission offices in New York. There are records to be kept for Health and Human Services, too. After lunch, you'll work in the kitchen helping with dinner preparations. The residents are not allowed on the second floor, so they won't see you in the office. You can take a back stairway to the kitchen, so your encounters with others should be few and far between."

Maddie had packed her underwear and Hawaiian garments in the same suitcase, and she put the other case in the closet without opening it. She put Linc's ring on a long silver chain and hung it around her neck. She arranged her clothes in the dresser drawers and sat down on the bed, feeling lonely.

Had Linc already learned that she was gone? Was he sad or angry? Probably a little of both.

TWELVE

When Ailina Zadok finished her work in the elementary school sponsored by the shelter, Stella accompanied her to the room and introduced Maddie to her as Madison Lee.

"I'll leave the two of you to get acquainted. Madison, your duties will start in the morning. Ailina, I'd appreciate it if you'll keep her secrets and take Madison under your wing until she finds her way around."

Ailina was a soft-spoken girl, and Maddie judged her roommate to be a few years older than she was. Hawaiian, Ailina had dark eyes but her complexion was light. A few inches taller than Maddie and several pounds heavier, she walked with a plodding gait.

"I'm pleased to have a roommate," she said. "I've been alone for over a month, and having come from a large family, I miss the companionship. You're volunteer help, I suppose. Will you be staying long?"

"I don't know how long I'll be here."

"It's almost time for dinner, so we can get acquainted later."

The dining room for the staff was in a room adjacent to the kitchen. The children and youth ate in a room on the opposite side of the kitchen.

"Mámá Stella always eats the evening meal with them," Ailina explained, "to give the rest of us a break."

Ailina was attentive in guiding Maddie through the buffet line, which had an adequate choice of food. She also introduced Maddie to the dozen or so other staff members.

Still affected by her separation from Linc, Maddie wasn't hungry, but she took portions of chicken and rice, baked corn and a vegetable salad. Ailina chose a table for two, and Maddie wondered if Stella had told Ailina to keep her separate from the other staff members.

When they returned to their room, Maddie sat on her bed, which looked more comfortable than the two straight chairs provided for them.

While Maddie filed her nails, she said, "Since we'll be together a lot, Stella suggested that I share my real identity with you. I'm Madison Lee Horton, and I came to Hawaii almost a month ago to visit Lincoln Carey, a friend of my father's."

Ailina's eyes opened wide, and she glanced at Maddie incredulously. "It's your father's death that the navy is investigating now?"

Maddie nodded, surprised, and a little distressed

that Ailina knew about it. She hadn't thought the investigation was so widely known.

"Oh, my," Ailina said, shaking her head. "I supposed you were a volunteer like others who've come from the mainland."

Maddie briefly explained her background and her reason for visiting Hawaii. "I thought this trip to Hawaii would be the most pleasant time of my life," Maddie said bitterly. "It's been anything but pleasant. Almost from the first, I've been threatened and intimidated, supposedly by my father's enemies."

"Shouldn't you leave Hawaii? That might help."

Maddie swallowed hard, and she looked away from Ailina's somber face. *Was this another warning?* Had she jumped out of the frying pan into the fire when she left Linc's home? Had she landed in the stronghold of her enemies? She knew nothing about these people with whom she'd cast her lot.

"I may leave soon, but in the meantime, I came here for safety," she answered, and her voice trembled slightly. "I'm not only afraid for myself, but my friends if they continue to shelter me."

"But didn't you consider that there might be danger to Open Arms Shelter if your enemies discover where you are now?"

Maddie felt like an errant child who'd been reprimanded. "Stella thought my disguise would keep anyone from knowing I'm here. No one knows who I am except you and Stella. She said it was safe to tell you. But if you're unhappy about my living here, I'll go to a hotel until I can make arrangements to leave Hawaii. I don't want people hurt because they help me."

"It really isn't any of my business," Ailina said. "I was thinking of Stella. She won't turn anyone away. She's often threatened by angry parents when she won't let them see their children, who've run away from an abusive home life."

The trauma of leaving Linc now coupled with finding she wasn't welcome at Open Arms Shelter stressed Maddie to the breaking point. She stood up and angrily snatched the wig from her head and removed her glasses.

When her blond hair tumbled over her shoulders, Ailina gasped. "You really do look like a different person with that disguise. I don't believe that anyone will recognize you. Your accent might betray you, but if you don't talk much, no one should suspect your identity. I'm sorry I said anything."

Maddie went into the small powder room, containing a toilet and a lavatory to remove her heavy makeup. She left the door ajar so they could talk.

"Actually, Stella chose this for me."

"Well, don't pay any attention to my comment," Ailina said. "If Stella wants to help you, I'll do my part."

Somewhat mollified, Maddie said, "I appreciate that. But that's enough about me. Tell me about yourself, Ailina."

"I'm a native of Maui—a student at the University of Hawaii. I work at the shelter for my room and board."

"What are you studying?"

"Basic subjects right now, but I want to go into missionary work of some kind. It will take several years for me to finish college, but I'll have to decide on a definite course of study before long."

Maddie massaged her face gently with some cream that Roselina had bought for her. "But in the meantime, I'd say that you're already doing missionary work by teaching here."

"That's true. We have some very sad cases."

"I haven't been to Maui yet. Linc planned to take me before I went home, but with the mystery hanging over me, I'm not in the mood for sightseeing. Before I left his house, I postponed my flight for the time being and e-mailed the university to cancel my classes for the winter semester. The future seems so insecure that I don't know what plans to make. I can't imagine why anyone would want to take my life over something that happened ten years ago."

"The Sanale family, who may be harassing you, are natives of the island of Hawaii, but they have family connections in Honolulu. I don't doubt that Kamu is being harbored by his relatives."

"There's been some speculation that the Sanale brothers broke out of prison because they'd heard I was coming to Hawaii. But Linc can't figure out how they knew I'd be visiting. There may be some connection between the Sanales and someone in his office. But it's still hard for me to believe that, because of what happened ten years ago, anyone would be determined to kill me."

"Unfortunately, we still have a few natives who follow what some Christians call black religion. These beliefs have been around since Hawaii's beginnings. After the missionaries came, in some areas there's been a mixture of Christianity and the ancient beliefs. Some people worship Kila, an ancient god, who was only a servant in a king's household, but he saved the king's life and was subsequently proclaimed to be a god. Then Kila was killed by his enemies, and the rule of a life for a life was instituted. In Hawaiian, we'd say, *he ola na he ola.* Adherents of the old ways mete out justice by killing a member of the family who've killed one of their relatives. The Sanale family may believe they must kill you to avenge their dead relatives."

"Gruesome. Hasn't the Christian message had any impact on Hawaii?"

"Some, of course. My family have been Christians for generations. But we have such a complex of cultures in the islands that it's hard to override ancient beliefs. I think the best thing for you to do is to go home."

"But wouldn't they pursue me to West Virginia?"

"It's unlikely. For one thing, it would be a very expensive trip, and Hawaiians would be very conspicuous in your state."

Unless they wore a disguise like I'm doing,

Maddie thought, wondering what she should do. Although she'd left for Linc's own good, Maddie missed him.

Linc spent a miserable two days before he heard from the investigator. He asked Ed Blake to report to him at home because Linc didn't want anyone to know that he'd hired the detective.

"Good news," Blake said as soon as he strolled into Linc's home office two days later. He didn't look like the bearer of good news, for his face was as lugubrious as an undertaker's at a funeral.

"Then you've found her!" Linc said, and silently thanked God for His mercies.

"You'll have to check it out, but I'm confident enough that I've already spent that extra five hundred dollars."

Ignoring Blake's idea of a joke, hope dawning in his heart, Linc asked quickly, "What have you learned?"

"She's using the name Madison Lee and staying at a mission in the midcity called Open Arms Shelter. I was sure she'd gone there, and I've been staked out for forty-eight hours trying to get a glimpse of her. This morning, two women came out the back door of the mission and walked down the street to a drugstore. One was definitely a native. The other one was dressed in Hawaiian clothes and she had short, dark hair. She had no resemblance to the angel in your photograph."

Blake shot one of his rare smiles toward Linc, who

felt his face flushing. Was there anyone in the state of Hawaii who didn't know he was in love with Maddie?

"But from the way she walked and the way she carried her shoulders," Blake continued, "I think she may be the one you're seeking. I accidentally bumped into her in the drugstore, and although she wore colored glasses, I think she has blue eyes."

Linc had heard of Open Arms Shelter. It was located in a questionable section of Honolulu, and he didn't like the idea of Maddie living there.

"How'd you come up with your facts?"

"I learned that a van with Open Arms Shelter on its side was seen leaving your driveway on the day Miss Horton disappeared. Also, there were some calls from your house to the mission and the international airport two days prior to Miss Horton's departure. I've had somebody watching the mission and airport around the clock since then. She didn't take a plane, so what do I do now?"

"Keep watch at the airport and the mission until I check on what you've learned this far. If I can be assured that she is at the shelter, I won't bother her for the time being. She might be safer there than here with me."

Linc stayed awake most of the night wondering how he could be sure Maddie was at Open Arms Shelter without going there. If her enemies were following him, he didn't want to lead them to her. But he had to know if she was living at the mission.

From a pay phone, he called Open Arms Shelter

the next morning before he went to the office. He had no idea what he would say when someone answered the phone. He couldn't believe his good fortune when a soft voice, that he would have known among a million, answered.

"Maddie?" he said experimentally.

No answer, but at least she didn't hang up.

"This is Linc. Are you all right? I have to know you're safe."

"How did you find me so fast?" she whispered.

"By hiring the best detective in Honolulu. I haven't been able to sleep or rest since I learned you were gone."

He heard her sniff, and she answered in a shaky voice, "Are you mad at me?"

"No. But I've been very worried—there are so many things that could have happened to you."

"I didn't want to leave, but when my enemies threatened *you,* I couldn't stay any longer. But I didn't want to go home, either. I canceled my flight and my university classes for this semester. I'd rather stay here and be in danger, than to go home and not know what's happening. They're shorthanded at the shelter, and I'm working to pay my way. I do think I'm of use."

"I miss you, and so does Roselina, and I'm not worried about the threat against me. But as long as your enemies don't know you're at the mission, you're probably safer than living with me. Just be careful. Can I call you occasionally?"

"I work in the office every morning and in the kitchen during the afternoon. You could call mornings, and if I can't talk, I'll tell you."

"We'll see what happens in a few days, and maybe I can come by some evening and take you out to dinner. In the meantime, if you have any trouble, you call me."

"I'm a brunette now, so you might not recognize me," she said, a trace of laughter in her voice. "I don't even recognize myself when I look in the mirror."

"My investigator told me that. I hope you didn't dye your hair."

"Oh, no. But I had to cut off a few inches so I could tuck it under the wig."

Wondering if it was a wise thing to do, but succumbing to his need to see Maddie, three days later, Linc called to ask Maddie if he could come to see her.

"I'd like to talk to Stella, too," he added.

"Why?"

"I suppose I just want to see if I think she can guard you well enough."

"I'll have to ask Stella if you can come. After all, she's taken me under her protection. Call back about noon."

Since Stella spent most of the morning with the residents of the shelter, it was after eleven before she came to the office. Maddie immediately told her about Linc's call.

Stella hesitated briefly before she said, "If your life is in danger, as you think, it seems to me that you're running a risk to go outside at all. You see what happened when you went to the drugstore with Ailina. If Mr. Carey's detectives recognized you, your enemies could, too."

Stifling her disappointment, Maddie said, "You're probably right. I'll tell him not to come."

Smiling slightly, Stella said, "But it really isn't for me to say. You and Mr. Carey are adults and should make, and be responsible for, your own decisions. You're under no obligation to stay here."

"He'd like to meet you, but we don't want to cause you any trouble."

"I live with trouble twenty-four hours a day, so a little more won't be a problem. Let me know what time Mr. Carey is coming, and I'll be available."

She hugged Maddie's shoulders gently. Maddie had a feeling that Stella also wanted to meet Linc.

Linc had been around Honolulu long enough that he was well-known in many sectors. The Sanale family might have him shadowed to lead them to Maddie, so he left his car in a parking garage he never frequented. He took a taxi to a midway point, walked a few blocks and caught another taxi to Open Arms Shelter. Maddie had told him to come to a side entrance that wasn't well lit and to knock three times.

He left the cab two blocks from the shelter, and told the driver to come back in a half hour. With his hand on the gun in his pocket, he walked furtively down the street. Maddie must have been waiting, for as soon as he knocked the door opened a few inches.

"Who is it?" a soft voice whispered.

"Linc."

She threw open the door, he entered quickly, and closed the door behind him. A woman he hadn't seen before looked up at him. He had trouble believing it was really Maddie.

"How could you have changed so much?" he said. He took her hand and pressed it against his cheek. "Blonde or brunette—I'm glad to see you."

"I've been so lonely," she said in a tear-smothered voice, adding, "Stella is waiting for us in the office on the second floor."

He followed her through the dim corridor and up the stairs admiring her lithe body. No wig or makeup could change her graceful walk. Stella opened the door when Maddie knocked.

Maddie introduced them, and Linc said, "I want to thank you for taking Maddie in. Since she's my guest, I feel responsible for her welfare. I'll be happy to pay for her housing. Until the police capture the man who's threatening her, she may be safer here than in my home."

Stella shook her head. "The work she's doing is a big help to us. Besides, Mr. Carey, our shelter is a haven for anyone in need."

Linc was impressed by the iron determination re-

flected in Stella Oliver's face—a valuable character-
istic for a woman who worked in the slums of
Honolulu.

"Thanks for letting me take her out for dinner."

Stella looked from him to Maddie, and a slight
smile crossed her face.

"You really don't need my permission. She's
probably safer not to go outside the mission at all,
but she needs a break. We lock the doors at nine
o'clock so you must return before then."

Linc looked at his watch. "That will give us a
little more than two hours." Turning to Maddie, he
said, "It's a little cool tonight. You might want to take
a sweater."

As soon as Maddie left, Linc said to Stella, "I
know it's obvious I'm in love with her, but I haven't
told her. I assure you that she's safe with me."

"I have no doubt of that, and I'm glad you stopped
by. I sensed from the note I received from my friend,
Caroline Renault, that she was concerned about
Maddie's visit. I'll be glad to report that Maddie is
in safe hands."

"Thanks. I'm doing my best, but a lot of problems
have come up that I can't seem to handle. It would
be easier if we could be given a map for the future."

"But that isn't the way God directs our lives. He
gave us a free will and the wisdom to make decisions. From that point, it's in our hands."

But when he loved Maddie so much, was he
capable of making a decision that was good for her?

* * *

Edena, disguised now as Kamu, stood in the shadow of the palm-covered shelter. The lapping of the waves on Waikiki Beach usually soothed her, but she had lost sight of her prey. She was angry. And the gods were angry at her.

The blood of her dead relatives cried out for revenge, and Edena's soul was weary of failure. She longed to join the rest of her family. But the blood price must be paid. Where had Madison Horton gone?

Hearing a quiet step behind her, knife in hand, she swung toward the sound. Recognizing the man, she said quietly, "Ah, Tivini, you're late."

"I couldn't find a taxi."

"What news do you have for me?"

"Nothing. The chit has disappeared. I think she's gone home."

"I think not. My cousins have watched planes departing for Houston since she left the Carey place. She is still in Hawaii. Your sister can tell you where she is."

"My sister doesn't know."

Steve wanted this investigation to stop. If he could persuade Edena that Madison was no longer in Hawaii, maybe she'd forget her plan of revenge. But he also knew that the death of Madison Horton would benefit him, too. He liked Madison, but he was a pragmatic man.

"My sister, too, believes that the Horton girl is still in Hawaii. She says that about a week ago, Linc

Carey seemed to stop worrying about where she is. Of course, that could mean he's learned she'd left Hawaii. If she's still here, if you shadow Carey, he'll eventually lead to Madison."

"*You* shadow him. I have plans to make for the sacrifice. I'll give you one week to find her and deliver her to me at this spot. If not, I will send the papers proving your involvement in the theft of equipment to the navy officers. For ten years you've been free while my family has done hard time and you're as guilty as they were."

"If you've got that proof," Tivini said with a sneer, "why haven't you used it before this?"

"Because my brothers figured to make you pay for our silence when they left prison." Edena laughed bitterly. "And you haven't amounted to anything. You can't even support yourself, let alone give us any money. So you're going to help me find Madison Horton!"

The urge to kill was strong in Tivini, and his hand tightened around the gun in his pocket. But he didn't have the nerve to use it. "I'll try to find her."

"You have one week. I'll be here three nights from now. Report on your progress."

THIRTEEN

Stella walked downstairs with them, and when she opened the door, she peered out cautiously. "Your cab is waiting."

When Linc followed Maddie into the taxi, he said to the driver, "Take us to a nearby reputable restaurant."

"How about the Pacific Grill ten blocks away? They have quick service and a wide selection of food."

"Just what we want," Linc said.

Linc put his arm around Maddie's waist and drew her close to him. She nestled contentedly in his arms.

"I guess I should apologize for stealing your ring," she said.

"You didn't steal it—you left your opal ring in its place, which I brought back to you. I know how much you prize your mother's ring." He took the ring out of his pocket and put it on her finger.

"Thank you. I have missed wearing the ring, but I wanted something of yours to take with me. I didn't feel quite so bad when I left mine in its place."

"You're welcome to the ring," he said, "but it's too big for you. Have it sized to your finger, if you like."

She pulled a chain from inside her dress. "I wear it on this chain."

Why had she wanted something of his? Did this mean that she missed him as much as he'd missed her in the past few days? But that wasn't a safe subject, so he said, "I like Stella. You'll be as safe there as anywhere, but I miss you in the house."

The questions he'd been considering for weeks flitted through his mind. If he missed her when she was still in Hawaii, how would he feel when she went back to the mainland? Should he ask her to stay with him?

"I didn't want to run away, but it wasn't fair for me to hide behind you. I didn't want you in danger."

"Ahonui admitted that she'd told you."

"I'm glad she did."

"Well, I'm not," he said sternly. "In the first place, she shouldn't listen to my personal messages. I'll admit there have been times when I've asked her to monitor my business calls. But, regardless, she had no right to pass that information on to you. When I confronted her with my suspicions, I warned her that if you came to harm, she could look for another job."

"Then I would have been responsible for that," Maddie said in a peevish tone.

He shook her slightly. "Ahonui brought that on herself. Stop blaming yourself for everything that happens."

"If I hadn't come to Hawaii, the Sanale family wouldn't know anything about me. Why wouldn't I blame myself if you're hurt or Carey Enterprises is disrupted because of me?"

"But I invited you to visit," he said sternly. "So, if we go by that reasoning, it would be my fault. The Sanales are crooks. If they'd stayed honest, none of this would have happened. Your father would still be alive. It's childish to blame yourself for something that started years ago."

The instant the words left his lips, Linc knew he'd pushed the wrong button. Although Maddie didn't move out of his embrace, her body stiffened. The atmosphere got so cold in the taxi, he thought he must have taken a sudden trip to the North Pole. Streetlights illuminated the car slightly, and he saw that her eyes blazed with anger.

She turned on him furiously. "I'm tired of having you treat me like a child. I *am not* a child. For your information, it's a maturing experience to lose your father when you're a child. And I grew up a lot during the five years I watched my mother die. It aged me considerably when I sat by her bed and watched her gasp for her last breath. I had to leave VOH when I was eighteen and started making my own decisions without any guidance from anyone. I can't help the way I look, but I hardly consider myself a child."

"I…" Linc started to defend himself, and Maddie interrupted him.

"Since the day I landed in Hawaii you've been

talking down to me as if I was still ten years old. You're my *self-appointed* guardian—I didn't ask you to look after me." She moved away from him. "Take me back to the shelter. If I go to dinner with you, you'll probably ask the waitress to put a bib around my neck so I won't spill anything on my clothes. And if once more, you talk to me as if I haven't been weaned, I'm apt to slap you."

She turned her face from him, but not before he noticed that her lips were trembling. Torn between amusement and chagrin, Linc swung her into the circle of his arms more roughly than he'd ever touched her before. When he lowered his head to hers, she tried to fend him off by pounding on his chest with both hands.

His lips brushed against hers as he said, "It would be much simpler for my peace of mind if I did think of you as a child."

His kiss was warm and sweet, and tended to cool her anger as words couldn't have done.

"But regardless of what we feel, I'm eleven years older than you are. That may not sound like much now, but it could seem like a lot more later on." He looked away from her. "You're forcing me to say things I shouldn't say."

Maddie's heartbeat skyrocketed, and momentarily she felt as if she was floating in space. She pulled away from him and moved to the far side of the taxi. After she caught her breath, she said, "I'm sorry I lost my temper. But I do want to go back to the shelter."

Suddenly aware that the taxi had stopped, Linc realized they were in front of the restaurant. The taxi driver was peering back at them, a smile on his lips.

"Well, buddy, here you are. I hated to interfere."

Embarrassed, Linc paid the fare and urged Maddie to go into the restaurant. "If we return immediately, Stella will know we've been quarreling. You don't want that, do you?"

Without answering, Maddie stepped out of the cab and preceded him into the restaurant. Her back was as rigid as a flagpole, and he knew she was still angry. He chose a corner booth where he could see all parts of the room, which he surveyed carefully to determine if they had created any particular notice. He had dressed as casually as he would have for a walk on the beach. Maddie's Hawaiian outfit was no different from the garments worn by the native women in the room. No one seemed to be watching them.

They ordered and sat silently. Maddie wouldn't look at him. She sipped on the water the waitress brought and played idly with the wrapped silverware.

Linc had seen Maddie display a lot of moods in the past month—pleasure, fear, love, optimism, but anger was a part of her that he hadn't anticipated. This new trait, coupled with the fact that he couldn't get used to her changed appearance made him uncomfortable.

Her beauty was in no way lessened by changing from a blonde to a brunette. When he'd first seen her, he'd thought she was the most beautiful woman he'd ever seen and that her appearance couldn't be improved. But the woman across the table from him was as alluring now as she'd ever been. So it wasn't her appearance that had drawn him to her, but rather her innate honesty, spiritual and moral character. These intangible qualities made Maddie what she really *was*. It was just an added touch when God made her beautiful.

Maddie had worn very little makeup—in fact her glowing ivory skin needed no enhancement. Now her makeup, expertly applied, had changed the color of her skin to a dusky tan. Linc hadn't believed that her eyes could be any more compelling, but with the dark eye shadow and the tinted glasses, she now had mysterious eyes that seemed almost black.

Never again would Maddie seem like a girl to him. Her altered appearance had changed her into an adult in his eyes. He'd been ashamed of himself the few times he'd kissed her, as if he was kissing the ten-year-old he'd remembered. In her disguise, she looked almost as mature as he was. He couldn't see one trace of the girl he'd known, and although he knew that he'd miss the child of his memory, he understood how much more this mature woman could mean to him. He felt no compulsion now about loving Maddie and seeking to make her love him, too. The very thought excited him.

This wasn't the time or the place to tell her of his discovery, so he said, "What are you doing to keep busy at the shelter?"

"Stella has given me private work where I won't be seen much by the residents. I spend the morning in the office, helping with correspondence. They have lots of reports to submit on each case, so I'm learning to do that. Actually, it's good experience—because of the needs I saw at VOH I've considered preparing for social work."

"I didn't know that. Since you're doing a history project, I assumed that history was a priority for you."

She shook her head. "The history class is an elective, for I hadn't gotten much history in my high school education. The school I attended before my mother died didn't offer United States history until the junior year. VOH scheduled history in the sophomore year, so I don't know much about the country's history."

Linc understood why Maddie was annoyed that he'd treated her like a child. Obviously she'd been making adult decisions for a long time.

"Stella doesn't want me to have any contact with the residents, so I work in the kitchen during the afternoons, cleaning up after lunch and helping to prepare dinner."

Her smooth, well-cared-for hands didn't indicate that she had done much manual work.

"That doesn't bother you?" Linc asked.

"Of course not. All of the residents at VOH had jobs assigned to them. We cleaned, cooked and worked in the gardens. Besides, I did most of the housework at home while my mother was sick. I'm not a spoiled brat, if that's what you think."

Linc sighed inwardly. Seemed as if every time he opened his mouth he put his foot in it. He was saved from answering when the waiter brought their food.

Maddie was so annoyed with herself that she felt like screaming. She had never talked to anyone as she had to Linc this evening. What on earth was wrong with her? She'd chided him for treating her like a child. Well, her behavior the past hour had certainly been childish.

Trying to repair the damage she'd done to their relationship, she said, "Stella reminds me a lot of Miss Caroline. She doesn't have as many residents as we had at VOH, but she doesn't have many full-time workers, either."

"How many residents are there?"

"They change every day, it seems, but I believe there are about thirty now."

They still had twenty minutes before nine o'clock when they finished dinner, but they soon found a taxi. When they got back to Open Arms Shelter, Linc walked with her to the door.

"Thank you for taking me out tonight," Maddie said, "but I believe it will be better for both of us if you stay away from me."

Linc felt as if he'd just landed in the Arctic Circle again. Her coolness and rejection confused him, and he glared at her. Did he deserve such treatment? If she expected him to grovel at her feet, he wouldn't. His temper flared, and his voice was cold when he answered, "Very well."

He made no move to touch her, but he stood at the door until she was inside and he heard the door lock. He bounded down the steps and entered the taxi. Why had he been so foolish as to invite Maddie to visit him?

Ailina was lying in bed, reading, when Maddie went to the room. She pitched the dark brown wig on her dresser and laid her glasses aside. She took off her dress and hung it in the closet. She went into the lavatory and removed the heavy coat of makeup she was obligated to wear every day. She was sick and tired of this disguise she wore. Actually, she was sick and tired of Hawaii and everything in it. She might as well go home. Was it necessary for her to stay in Hawaii until she learned whether her father had been murdered or had died an accidental death? He was gone and nothing could change that. What could she personally do to find those responsible and bring them to justice? She knew now that she'd used this investigation as a reason for staying in Hawaii so she could be near Linc. But what did it matter now?

She could probably get a flight home in a few days. But what would she do then? It was too late to continue her college classes for the quarter. Perhaps she could get a job of some kind until the next semester started. She'd made a mess of everything.

Laying aside her book, Ailina asked, "Want to talk?" when Maddie got into bed, hooked her hands behind her neck and stared into space.

"No, not really. I've talked too much already tonight."

Ailina shrugged her shoulders, switched off the reading light and turned on her side away from Maddie.

So now she'd made Ailina mad! Why was she such a shrew tonight? She supposed she'd turn on Stella next. She turned off the lights so she wouldn't disturb Ailina's sleep, flexed her knees and laid her head on her knees.

God, what is wrong with me? I've always believed that You are my Guide and Protector. I still believe that, but since I've been in Hawaii, I've been on a roller coaster of emotions. Help me to understand Your will for my life.

Praying calmed her somewhat, but when she stretched out under the covers, she couldn't go to sleep.

An hour later, a light tap on the door alerted Maddie. She slipped quietly out of bed and cracked the door, without removing the security chain.

Stella stood at the door, fully clothed. Maddie opened the door immediately, surprised at Stella's agitation. She was always steady and in charge of any situation. Tonight, there was a wild look in her eyes, and her voice trembled, "I'm sorry to wake you," she said, "but I need Ailina for an emergency."

"She's asleep. I'll be glad to help you."

"Ailina has had a hard day. If you don't mind, come along," Stella said, turned abruptly and hurried down the hallway.

Maddie shrugged into a robe and tied it securely

around her waist. She picked up her slippers, turned out the light and eased out of the room and locked it behind her. She put on her slippers and hurried toward the stairway. Stella had already disappeared, and Maddie didn't know where to go.

She groped her way down the dimly lit stairway and paused before the door to the right at the foot of the stairs, which led to the resident hall for those who spent the night at the shelter. A shiver of panic shook Maddie and she wondered if she was exposing herself to discovery. But Stella had guarded her carefully—surely she wouldn't have accepted her help if there was any danger.

Maddie pushed on the door, which opened easily. An attendant sat inside an enclosed cubicle directly inside the door. She lifted startled eyes. Maddie opened her mouth to ask the woman where to find Stella, when a bloodcurdling shriek sounded and goose bumps riddled Maddie's flesh.

Trying to steady her erratic pulse, Maddie ran in the direction of the shriek. She hurried into an anteroom of an outside entrance Maddie had never used.

Two policemen held a struggling, shouting girl, who looked to be in her early teens. Her Asian features were covered with makeup. She wore a bikini underneath a long, transparent gown. The girl ranted in a language Maddie didn't understand, and her eyes were wild. Holding a medical syringe, Stella stood beside the girl, speaking soothingly.

Shaking herself out of her astonishment, Maddie said, "I'm here. What can I do?"

Stella handed Maddie the syringe. "Hold this until I can calm her down. I can't risk giving her an injection when she's carrying on like this."

Stella took the child's flailing hands and held them closely in hers. The girl kicked out savagely, and her high-heeled shoes cracked Stella's ankle. Stella flinched slightly, but she kept whispering quietly, calmly to the child.

Maddie leaned against the wall to support her trembling legs. She wouldn't be much help to Stella if she passed out. At VOH, she hadn't been subjected to this type of horror because residents were emotionally able to live in a communal situation before they were accepted. This was a raw side of life she'd never known before.

Gradually, the child quieted and her head drooped sideways. Stella held out her hand, and Maddie gave her the syringe.

"Get some blankets out of the closet in the room next door," she said quietly.

Maddie welcomed something to do. She groped along the dark hallway until she saw a sign that indicated a storeroom. She opened the door and felt along the wall for a light switch, all the time wondering if someone was in the darkness waiting to grab her.

She found the switch and turned on the low-wattage light. Several shelves held cleaning and bathroom supplies, but she didn't see any bedcovers.

She found them in a closet and gathered three blankets into her arms.

When she returned to the anteroom, the child lay on a couch. The sedative must have been having an effect for she had ceased struggling, but her tiny fingers moved restlessly and she groaned, perhaps from mental anguish. Stella took the blankets from Maddie and tenderly wrapped them around the child.

The two policemen stood in the background, and when Maddie glanced their way, one of the men stared at her intently. She turned her back, and as she did her long blond hair fell forward over her face. She lifted her hand and touched her face, realizing that she was no longer disguised.

At the same time, Stella rose from her knees and looked at Maddie. The horror on her face alerted Maddie to the fact that Stella, too, had just now discovered that Maddie's presence at Open Arms Shelter was no longer secret.

The police sergeant said, "Do you think you can handle the situation now?"

"Yes," Stella answered. "We'll do what we can. If you gentlemen will come with me to the office, we'll take care of the paperwork." She turned to Maddie, and perhaps hoping to undo any harm that might have occurred, she said, "Miss Lee, will you stay with her until I come back?"

As the three left the anteroom, the shorter policeman took another searching look at Maddie. She sank into a chair close to the girl, wondering what to do if she became violent again. While she waited, Maddie also worried about her own situation. Had that policemen recognized her?

When Stella returned, she said, "I surely made a mistake when I let you come here to help tonight. I didn't realize you weren't in disguise."

"I was already in bed when you came, and I didn't think about it, either. One of those cops kept looking at me. He must have recognized me."

Stella smiled. "You probably don't realize what a fetching picture you made tonight—almost anyone would have stared. You have on that white robe, and with your blond hair tumbling about your shoulders, the young man probably thought you were an angel. I'm not surprised that he stared. I only hope that was his *only* reason for looking at you."

The girl on the couch stirred and coughed.

"Who is she?" Maddie whispered. "Why did they bring her here?"

"This is her third time at the shelter. That's the reason she was putting up such a fight. She's a twelve-year-old child on drugs and has taken to prostitution to feed her habit. The police know her now and pick her up every time they see her. The other two times, we've kept her a few days, but we aren't equipped to cure her of this addiction. We've turned her over to the custody of her father, but he beats her to make her straighten up. That never works. This time, I'm going to keep her until she can be admitted to a clinic where she can get some help. She's suicidal, and I can't risk turning her away again."

"Does she come from a poor family?"

"No. Her father is a businessman in Honolulu, but his wife left him, and he doesn't give the child any care at all. I don't usually go this far in helping children, but we have some volunteer lawyers who assist us. I'll see if one of them will take steps to remove this child from his care."

"You're doing wonderful work here. Tell me a bit about your background and why you chose to come to Honolulu."

"My home is in North Dakota, but I had several misfortunes in my life. I had two miscarriages and my husband died about the time my church denomination started this mission. I'm a nurse by profession, and to get away from my own troubles, I volunteered to come as a short-term missionary. That was thirty years ago. I've been here ever since," she added with a half smile.

"How did you meet Miss Caroline?"

"Her mother and mine grew up together in the same town, and they kept in touch after my family moved. Caroline and I corresponded often, and after my husband died, I went to VOH to visit her. Seeing the work she was doing encouraged me to accept a position at Open Arms Shelter."

"I'm been thinking of going into social work, partly because of Miss Caroline's example. Being here with you these few days has made me feel it's the thing for me to do."

"It may be, but you want to be really sure. Both Caroline and I wanted to be a wife and mother—and there's no greater calling than that. I may be talking out of turn, but you have a young man who seems very interested in you, and I've gathered you feel the same way about him."

Maddie's consternation must have shown on her face, for Stella said, "I'm sorry—I shouldn't have meddled. I don't have that right."

Coming on top of everything else that had happened tonight, this was more than Maddie could handle, and she started sobbing. Stella was beside her immediately and tried to soothe her.

"I'm going home," Maddie said. "That policeman may have recognized me, and I have no other place to hide. If the news gets out that you're harboring me, my enemies might start attacking the shelter. I'm a nuisance to everyone. I've got a return ticket, and it will be best for all concerned if I leave the islands."

"Maddie, don't make any rash decisions. You might make a mistake that will ruin the rest of your life. Pray about any move you make."

Maddie went back to her room and she tried to pray, but the words wouldn't come.

The next morning she called the airport. With a heavy heart she booked a flight for the following Monday.

FOURTEEN

When Linc got home after the disastrous evening with Maddie, he changed into swimming trunks, went to the beach and battled the waves until he was exhausted. The water chilled him, but he stretched out on the sand and stared toward the sky.

How could he make peace with Maddie? All he'd wanted to do was to protect her from himself. She deserved a younger man, and he hadn't wanted her to feel obligated to return his attentions if she regarded him as if he was her father. For all the innocence mirrored on her face, Maddie was obviously a deep thinker, and he hadn't been able to tell what she thought about him. Was it possible that she loved him?

Regardless, he'd really ruined it tonight. When he'd reprimanded her, was he acting like a father? But he didn't know how a father was supposed to act. The waves lapped at his feet as he prayed.

God, what's Your will for our lives? Is it right for Maddie and me to be together? Does she love me as a father or as a potential husband? I have all the questions, but You have the answers. Reveal them to me. My gut feeling is if I let Maddie go, I will have made the worst mistake of my life. Am I right?

He didn't get an immediate answer to his questions, but God did send peace of mind, so when he returned to the house, he felt comforted. Believing that God would work His will in their lives, he went to sleep and rested.

When Linc went to the office the next morning, Steve Kingsbury was in Ahonui's office. Linc hadn't seen Steve since Christmas Day, and he was surprised at the difference in the man. He looked haggard to the point that Linc said, "Anything wrong, Steve?"

Laughing hollowly, Steve answered, "Just too much work and too many late nights. I may go away for a vacation before too long."

Steve had always been shifty-eyed, but he wouldn't meet Linc's eyes at all. Linc figured Steve was putting the touch on his sister for a loan. He'd often suspected that Ahonui financed her brother, but he'd never inquired. It wasn't any of his business how Ahonui spent her money.

He went on toward his office, but halted his steps when Steve said, "Have you heard from Miss Horton since she returned home?"

How was he going to answer this without lying? But since Maddie hadn't gone home, he could answer in the negative.

He turned to face Steve, who was looking at the floor.

"No."

"I'm sure you must miss her," Steve persisted.

"Of course, I do," Linc said. "If you'll excuse me, I have a busy day ahead. I'll be away for a few days," he said to Ahonui. "I'm leaving this afternoon for Kauai and Maui."

He cast a questioning glance in Steve's direction, but Kingsbury wouldn't meet his eyes. Linc went into his office and closed the door. He stared at the walls for several minutes. Was there a hidden meaning in Steve's comments?

Later, as he drove to the airport, Linc considered calling Maddie to apologize before he left. After he parked his car, he picked up his cell phone. With a sigh, he put it in his briefcase. It would be better if he waited until he came back before he contacted her. They'd both been angry when they parted, and they needed a cooling-off period. But as he pointed his plane toward Maui, he regretted that he hadn't made the call.

Maddie had expected Linc to call her, and when he didn't, she was tempted to contact him. She wanted to apologize for the way she'd acted. She didn't dare call the office or his home for either Ahonui or Roselina would recognize her voice. Why hadn't she learned his cell-phone number? She wanted to hear his voice once more before she left Hawaii.

She had apologized to Ailina for her churlish

behavior, but Ailina assured her she hadn't been offended.

Perhaps sensing that Maddie was troubled, Ailina said, "I'm going home for the weekend, why not come with me? You haven't been to Maui, and it's the best of the islands. Although I'm undoubtedly prejudiced," she said, a smile lighting her somber features.

For a moment Maddie was tempted, but she finally decided that she shouldn't leave the shelter until she went to the airport to catch her plane. But she anticipated a long weekend.

Feeling lonely in the room without Ailina, Maddie was restless, and she couldn't go to sleep. She kept Linc's ring around her neck all the time, but she'd forgotten to remove her mother's ring. It kept twisting on her finger. She finally took it off and slipped it under the pillow.

Maddie didn't realize she'd gone to sleep until a noise woke her. At first, she felt disoriented. Struggling awake, it dawned on her that someone was knocking on the door. The clock showed two o'clock in the morning. She figured Stella must need help again, for the young girl she'd taken in a few nights ago was still violent. Stella stayed at her side most of the time.

Maddie padded to the door in her bare feet, but left the security chain on when she gapped the door.

"Who is it?"

"Steve Kingsbury. I need to talk to you."

Stunned to silence for a few minutes, she wondered how Steve had gotten inside Open Arms Shelter, especially at this hour of night. But since she associated Steve with Ahonui and Linc, she said in alarm, "What do you want?"

"It's about Linc. He's been hurt."

Linc! He'd said the magic word, and forgetting caution, Maddie unhooked the chain and opened the door. When she stepped back, Steve entered and closed the door.

"What happened?"

"He was returning from Kauai, and when he tried to land, his plane missed the runway. He's in the hospital. Ahonui is with him, but he's asking for you."

She gasped, smothering a shiver of panic.

"Is he going to die?"

"I don't know. I haven't seen him. Ahonui called me and told me to contact you."

"But how did you know where to find me?"

"Linc told her where you were."

Her instincts told her not to trust Steve, but as far as she knew, only Stella, Ailina and Linc, knew where she was hiding. A wave of apprehension spread through her. Linc's condition must be bad for him to reveal her whereabouts.

"If you'll step outside, I'll dress and go with you. I'll have to tell Stella where I am."

"Oh, she knows," Steve said casually. "I cleared it with her before I came to your room."

If Maddie hadn't been so distressed about Linc, she would have realized how hollow this story sounded. Steve turned toward the door, and Maddie said, "I'll not be long."

She turned her back on him, and he grabbed her from behind, and clapped his hand over her mouth. She struggled against him, and he said, *"Hele mai."*

Maddie knew that meant come in, and she heard the door open. Steve swung her to face the newcomer— a native Hawaiian, whom she recognized immediately as the person who'd been stalking her. Maddie felt a prick in her arm and she was out like a light.

INTERLUDE

A smile of satisfaction crossing her face, Edena watched as Tivini, Steve to most people, lowered the sedated blonde to the bed and trussed her up like a goose ready for the oven.

Determining which side of the room was Maddie's, she emptied the drawers of the chest, pulled all the garments from the closet and stuffed them in Maddie's luggage. When she thought she'd removed all traces of the girl from the room, she propped a typewritten note on the empty dresser.

Mama Stella,
Thank you for doing me the honor of sheltering me. I do not want to cause any trouble for you, so I must leave you. I go home in few days, so I hide until then. Tell Linc goodbye for me.
Madison.

Pleased with her handiwork, Edena peered out the door. The hallway was empty, and she motioned for Tivini to go first. He lifted the unconscious girl and crept out of the room. Edena picked up the two suitcases and followed him down the back steps and out the door, left conveniently open by a friendly cop who was a Sanale cousin. ·

Her departed family could rejoice tonight. Soon their deaths would be avenged.

FIFTEEN

To his annoyance, it had been necessary for Linc to delay his departure from Maui an extra day. Circling the small private airport in Honolulu waiting clearance for landing, he struggled to keep a tight rein on his emotions. He was worried about Maddie, and he didn't know why.

If he'd entered the shelter's phone number in his cell phone, he would have called Maddie the first day he was gone. But he didn't have the number, so he'd worried away the days, while one irritating business matter after another kept him from coming home.

He taxied toward his hangar and turned the plane over to a mechanic for servicing. When he got in his car, he drove a few blocks from the airport, pulled into a shopping center parking lot, found a bank of phones, looked up the shelter's number in the directory and dialed. It was only eleven o'clock, so Maddie should still be working. The phone rang and rang. Finally a man answered the phone and Linc stifled his disappointment.

"May I speak to Miss Lee?" he asked, remembering at the last minute that Maddie didn't use her family name at the center.

"She ain't here," he said. "This is Luke, the janitor. I'm sweeping the office."

"Will you call Miss Lee to the phone?"

"I tell you—she ain't at Open Arms Shelter anymore."

A sinking feeling in his stomach, Linc strove for patience, and said, "Then please get Stella for me."

"I'll see if I can find her."

Linc waited a full ten minutes, which seemed like an eternity, before Stella's voice came over the line.

"Yes?"

"Stella, this is Linc Carey. Where has Maddie gone?"

"I don't know. She went last night without telling me. She left a note, saying she was going home in a few days. All her clothes are gone. I don't know what to make of it." She explained about the people who'd seen Maddie without her disguise. "I suppose she thought the word would get around that she was staying here."

"Haven't you tried to find her?"

"No. Maddie is a competent woman. She made her move to Open Arms Shelter without any help when she thought you were in danger. I figure she left here for the same reason. I don't have a clue where to look."

A chill black wave of anxiety swept over Linc.

"Do you mind if I come and look at the note she left and at her room?"

"She did say goodbye to you in the note, so you can look at it if you like. I'm sorry not to be more helpful, but one of our residents committed suicide yesterday. We're in an upheaval around here now—police and social workers all over the place."

"I'm sorry I bothered you at such a time, but I'll come and see what I can find. I feel responsible for her."

With a sinking suspicion that Maddie hadn't walked away voluntarily this time, Linc wended his way through the crowded Honolulu streets. He had to show his identification to the officer on duty at the front door of the shelter, momentarily wondering why there was so much security over a suicide.

He asked for Stella, and she soon came and took him to Maddie's room and unlocked the door. She had such a worried look that he said, "Is there anything I can do?"

"No, I'm just distressed over this situation. We admitted a young girl a few nights ago. She was on drugs and we were making arrangements to send her to a drug rehab center. She was shot yesterday. We thought it was suicide, although I couldn't imagine where she would have gotten the gun, for she didn't bring it in with her. Now the police are treating the case as a homicide, suspecting her father may have had her killed."

She opened the door into an austere room, which contrasted poorly to the room Maddie had occupied at his home. She had made quite a sacrifice for his safety.

"Another one of our staff members sleeps on the right side. Her things are still here." Stella pointed to an unmade bed. "As you can see, everything has been removed from Maddie's side. We've been in such turmoil that we haven't even made her bed."

Linc looked at the empty bed and closet with a sinking heart. He experienced again the lonely bereft feeling that had threatened to overwhelm him when he learned that Maddie had moved out of his house.

"What time did she leave?"

"I can't tell you. Ailina, Maddie's roommate, was away for the weekend, so Maddie was alone in the room. And with the shooting of the girl in the dormitory about midnight, we were all disorganized. It was midmorning before I knew Maddie was gone. I'm sorry I wasn't more attentive to her."

Linc put his arm across Stella's slumping shoulders. "Don't blame yourself. You couldn't watch her all the time."

The note was still propped on the dresser and Linc picked it up. He read it twice before he asked, "Does this sound like Maddie to you? She wouldn't have signed it Madison. Was it written on the computer in your office?"

Stella reached for the note. "As I told you, I've been so distraught since this child's death that I couldn't concentrate on this note. But you're right, it doesn't sound like Maddie. You can go to the office and check out the computer font if you want to. It's on this floor at the end of the hall, and the door is open."

"Did there seem to be any kind of struggle?"

"The room is just as I found it. I'm as concerned about Maddie as you are, but I have a police detective waiting to talk to me. Are you through in here?"

"No. I'd like to look around, if you don't mind. Are you going to report Maddie's disappearance to the police?"

"I don't think I should until I know she has disappeared. If she's gone into hiding—for her own protection—we should let it go for now. Stay as long as you want to, but please lock the door when you leave."

Linc agreed, and he sat on the low bed where Maddie had slept. He smelled the scent of the body lotion Roselina had given Maddie for Christmas. He'd learned to associate the scent with Maddie in the few days she'd stayed in the house.

The top sheet and blanket were folded neatly, just as Maddie would have done when she'd stepped out of bed. If there had been a struggle of any kind, the covers would have been disarranged. The pillow showed plainly where Maddie's head had rested.

Feeling more desolate than he had since his parents had died, Linc picked up the pillow and hugged it to him. Was the faint scent of her body lotion all that he had left of Maddie? He closed his eyes, a dull ache in his heart, as he wondered if he would ever see her again.

Shaking himself out of his lethargy, he opened his

eyes. Instead of moping around in her bedroom, he had to find her. He refused to believe that Maddie was lost to him. As he stood, he noticed an object that had been under the pillow.

Her mother's ring!

Maddie would never have left it behind. This fortified his conviction that Maddie had been taken against her will! He picked up the ring, kissed it and dropped it in his pocket, now galvanized into action.

He locked the door behind him, rushed down the stairs and into his car. He first telephoned Claudia Warren, the detective with the Hawaii State Police, and reported on Maddie's disappearance. She promised to check on the Sanale family members in the city. She would also talk to the officers who'd investigated the homicide at Open Arms Shelter to see if there was any connection.

He next telephoned Ed Blake, the detective who'd found Maddie before. He intended to spare no expense in finding Maddie. He knew now that all he'd accomplished in his life would count for nothing if Maddie was lost to him.

Maddie's head hurt. She couldn't understand why her mother didn't come and help her. And she was sick at her stomach, too. The bed was swaying back and forth. The mattress seemed damp. Why had her mother left her alone?

Maddie opened her eyes and instead of seeing the ceiling of her childhood bedroom, stars shone over her head. And she wasn't in a bed, but lying on the deck of a motorboat. The boat, swaying back and forth in the oncoming tide, agitated her squeamish stomach.

When her eyes adjusted to the semidarkness, she saw two men on the seats in front of her. When she heard the soft voice of Steve Kingsbury, Maddie remembered what had happened.

Linc! her heart cried, but she couldn't speak, finding her mouth was sealed with duct tape. Her hands and feet were tied, too. Was Linc really hurt, or had that been Steve's ruse to get her to open the door?

He certainly hadn't taken her to the hospital as he'd indicated, so she consoled herself that the rest of his story must have been a lie, too. Linc had told her he would be away a few days on business, but how long ago had that been? Praying that Steve's story had been fabricated to get his hands on her, she wondered how he was mixed up in the threat to her life. Was Ahonui also her enemy? Was it possible that Ahonui and her brother were involved with the Sanales?

The way she'd agreed, without hesitation, to go with Steve when she thought Linc was wounded, convinced Maddie beyond any doubt that she loved him. And remembering his kiss in the taxi the last night she'd seen him, she believed he loved her, too. Surely they could work through his doubts about the differences in their ages. Maddie realized that she looked as immature as a baby, but life had dealt her a lot of rough knocks and she'd learned to deal with them.

How she wished she hadn't been so quarrelsome the night Linc had taken her to dinner! Her attitude was really foreign to her true nature, and she would try to convince Linc that she hadn't meant what she'd said. That is, if she had the opportunity to see him again. Tears trickled from her eyes, and with her hands tied behind her back, she could do nothing about it.

Was she in the hands of the Sanale family? Had she been kidnapped by the ones who sought to avenge the death of their family members? Maddie feared that was the situation.

Where was she anyway? The boat wasn't moving. The two people were talking louder now, and Maddie's mind was more alert, so she concentrated on their words.

"Daylight is a long time coming this morning," one complaining voice said. Maddie didn't think it was a male voice. A few times she'd thought the person shadowing her was a woman; other times, she'd decided it was a man. Could her stalker have been the same person but in different disguises, as she herself had changed appearances?

"No longer than any other time," Steve said. "You're just impatient."

"Yes, impatient to fulfill the obligation to my family."

"You have other family members, why did you take on this vendetta single-handedly?"

"Because it is *my* father, *my* brothers who have died. I have cousins who have helped, but it is *I,*

Edena, who will wield the knife. It is I who will satisfy the souls of my loved ones."

"There are too many Coast Guard patrol boats passing by to suit me," Steve observed. "If one of them stops to see why we're sitting here, we're in trouble. The way seems clear now. You've got radar on this tub, and it should help us if we get lost. Let's get out of here."

"Don't get impatient, Tivini. I'll not take a chance on wrecking the boat. I've never learned to swim."

Shortly, however, Edena started the engine and revved the motor. Steve loosed the rope to the dock and jumped on board as the boat eased out into the open water of the Pacific. Maddie saw Diamond Head as they circled the island of Oahu, and she knew that wherever they were taking her, Linc was being left behind.

The spray of the water dampened her clothes, and the blanket they'd wrapped around her was scant protection. Her body was numb from being tied hand and foot. She longed for a drink of water, but gagged as she was, she couldn't get their attention. She pretended to be asleep, hoping to hear more.

"She should be awake by now," Steve said. "Are you sure that sedative wasn't stronger than you said?"

"She'll come around soon. I didn't want her to wake until after we left Oahu."

Despite her discomfort, the hum of the motor and the splashing waves lulled Maddie to sleep. She woke up when the motor nudged into a dock. Steve secured the boat and came to Maddie's side. Her contempt for him must have shown in her eyes as he loosened her bonds and lifted her from the boat, for he wouldn't meet her glance.

When he stood her on her feet, Maddie crumpled to the rocky beach. She had no feeling in her legs, but she struggled to sit up and when she started rubbing her legs, sharp burning pain coursed through her limbs. She could barely refrain from crying out as the blood started circulating in her arms and legs. They hadn't yet loosened her gag, and she figured they didn't intend to until they got her to wherever they were taking her.

They were on a rocky strip of land. Behind them was a steep, rugged incline, barren except for a mass of scrubby vegetation and a few trees. Maddie watched as Steve's companion, who was unmistakably a woman, piled brush over the boat and the dock.

"Are you able to stand now?" Steve asked, and she nodded.

He gave her a hand and she stood. Holding to his arm, she walked a few steps back and forth.

"You'll have to climb this mountain. I'll loosen the gag so you can eat and drink, but if you yell out, I'll bash you over the head. Do you promise to keep quiet?" Steve asked.

Maddie nodded, wondering who would hear her if she did yell. She couldn't see any indication that the area was inhabited.

The woman stood at a distance, peering up and down the coast. Maddie closed her eyes when the woman took her two suitcases from the boat. She rummaged in one bag and took out Maddie's tennis shoes, a pair of jeans and a shirt. She then tied rocks to the suitcases and threw them into the ocean. There went all the Christmas gifts she'd received from Linc, even the black pearls she'd cherished. She felt for the chain around her neck, grateful that she still had his ring.

Steve removed the gag, and she rubbed her numb lips, which felt as if she'd spent the day in a dentist's chair. He handed her a bottle of water, and she drank deeply, although a lot of the liquid ran over her face because her numb lips wouldn't function properly.

When Steve handed her a sandwich, Maddie said, "How'd you get mixed up in this anyway? Are you a member of the Sanale family?"

"No comment," he said. "I'm not in charge here."

The woman plodded toward them. Her face distorted with anger, she stared at Maddie, who refused to lower her gaze from the woman's malevolent stare.

"Do you know who I am?" she asked, an accent in her voice that Maddie hadn't noticed among the other Hawaiians.

"No, but I have seen you stalking me." She thought it might be dangerous to be impertinent with this woman, but even if they killed her, and she couldn't really think this would happen, she was determined to die bravely.

Pounding on her flat chest, she said, "I'm Edena, last member of my branch of the Sanale family. My brothers both died from wounds received in the prison break. When Kamu died before he could make you pay for the deaths of our father and brother, I vowed to uphold the honor of the Sanale family."

"Is it honorable to kill me? I was a mere child, living thousands of miles from here, when my father did his duty by revealing the crimes of your family."

Edena slapped Maddie's cheek so hard her head snapped backward.

"You lie! My family did not commit crime. The United States government had no right to annex Hawaii. Everything here belongs to the natives— they had a right to take the items."

Her stinging face convinced Maddie that she needed to control her tongue. She said nothing more. Edena threw Maddie's shoes and clothes at her feet and motioned for her to put them on. Maddie knew they wouldn't let her out of their sight, so she walked a distance down the coast, turned her back and hurriedly got out of the gown and robe. She put on the jeans and shirt and sat on a rock to tie her shoes, wishing she had a pair of socks. She carried her nightclothes with her when she returned to her captors. Edena snatched them out of her grasp, shredded them with her large hands and threw them in the water.

Steve picked up a backpack and strapped it over his shoulders. He tenderly replaced the gag in Maddie's mouth, and the way his hands trembled, she had the feeling he was sorry he was mixed up in her abduction. Thinking he might be an ally in her escape, Maddie decided to give him no trouble.

"Which way?" he asked.

Edena motioned to a narrow path that wound out of sight up the mountain. "I'll go first. You follow the woman."

Whatever Steve's role was in this abduction, it was apparent that Edena was in charge. Feeling like a lamb being led to the slaughter, Maddie took the walking stick Steve handed her.

Edena motioned imperiously for Maddie to follow her, and she took the first step on a path, wondering if it would lead to her death. She definitely believed that death and life was in God's hands, and that Edena couldn't take her life until God was ready for her to join Him in Heaven. Had she finished the work God had put her on Earth to do?

She didn't fear death, but her heart cried "Oh, Linc, if only we could have had more time together."

SIXTEEN

The path was rocky and steep, and even Edena found it necessary to stop often to rest. During one rest stop, they had a view of the ocean. Maddie looked down on the national park Linc had taken her to visit. She realized then, with a sinking feeling that they were no longer on Oahu, but on the island of Hawaii. She had no doubt that Linc wouldn't overlook anything in trying to locate her, but the islands covered a vast area, how could he know where she was?

The sun beamed on their backs before they were halfway up the mountain, and when Maddie thought she couldn't take another step, Edena called a halt. Maddie collapsed to the ground, realizing why they'd gagged her. Several buildings were visible on the mountain now that the haze had lifted, so they were in a populated area. The gag added to her discomfort, because it was much harder to breathe when she couldn't open her mouth.

"No yelling," Edena said as Steve removed the gag, a statement that amused Maddie. She was too tired to whisper, let alone yell. She drank half the water from the bottle Steve handed her in one long swallow. The cheese sandwich was dry, but it helped restore Maddie's energy, and she finished the rest of the water. She peeled a banana he gave her and lay back on the rough ground. At the moment, she didn't much care what happened to her. She closed her eyes.

Steve shook her awake, and she sat up, wondering how long they'd rested. When she stretched her legs, Maddie's aching muscles let her know they hadn't rested long enough. Edena stood adjusting her backpack, and Steve, too, was ready to travel. He helped Maddie to stand. For the most part, Edena ignored her, but Steve seemed inclined to make the climb as easy as possible for her.

Maddie's feet were swollen and burning spots on her heels indicated blisters. She limped a few steps and glanced upward. Vegetation hid the top of the mountain, and she wondered how much farther they had to climb.

Occasionally, to the right, Maddie saw the ocean and at one rest spot, she had another good view of Pu'uhonua o Hōnaunau National Park. Tears stung her eyelids as she remembered her day there with Linc. She thought of how he'd rededicated his life to God's service. A slight shiver tingled down her spine, recalling how she'd imagined herself fleeing to that ancient place of refuge. Her hope revived for a moment, thinking if she could escape from Edena, the woman would probably be superstitious enough not to kill her if Maddie could get to the place of refuge.

They'd almost reached the top of the mountain by midafternoon. Maddie feared that whatever was going to happen would be soon. Had the woman brought her up here, intending to push her off a cliff into the ocean? Maddie couldn't remember ever being so weary. Her back ached between her shoulder blades. She felt drained, lifeless. She walked with her head down, forcing one foot after another.

She didn't know that Edena had stopped until she bumped into the woman.

"Stop," she said, and grabbing Maddie's arm, she pulled her into the shelter of a grove of mango trees. "Hide, quickly," she called to Steve. He sprinted for cover behind a large boulder.

"What is it?" he called.

Edena pointed upward. "I don't like all these helicopters I've been hearing for the past hour. We're high enough now that I could see the markings on that last one. It was a state police chopper."

"You think they're looking for us?" Steve asked uneasily.

"That's what I'm wondering. I don't know how they could possibly be on to us, but let's stay hidden for a while. We're almost at our destination."

Another helicopter flew over, and Steve called, "That's a Coast Guard craft. They're looking for something. What are we going to do?"

"Stay hidden in the brush. Keep close together."

In order to stay hidden, they had to climb over boulders and through prickly underbrush. Maddie slipped once and scratched both knees. Blood trickled down her legs and into her shoes. When she stumbled and was too weary to get up, Edena grabbed her arm and pulled her several more feet into the entrance of a cave.

Maddie gasped when she noticed the alcoves in the wall of the cave, each holding a bundle that she suspected contained bones. Maddie immediately noticed a sickening smell, no doubt decaying flesh. *This was undoubtedly the mausoleum of the Sanale family.* If she'd had any doubts before, Maddie had none now. She was slated for death.

Maddie leaned against the wall of the cave and slid to a lounging position. Steve opened his pack and gave her a chunk of bread and another bottle of water. He sat down not far from Maddie and devoured a portion of the coarse bread.

Maddie had been hungry, but the acrid scent of her surroundings had taken her appetite. She forced herself to eat, watching as Edena walked from one alcove to the other. She stood by each one, her hand on the bundle of bones and wailed, *"He Ola na he ola,"* before she moved on to another.

"What's she saying?" Maddie asked.

Steve didn't answer.

"Tell me. I might as well know."

"A life for a life."

"Doesn't leave much doubt about what she plans for me, does it?"

With admiration in his voice, Steve said, "I'll have to admit you're a plucky woman. If I was going to be the sacrifice, I'd be howling to high heaven."

"And what makes you think you won't be sacrificed, too," she said quietly. "I heard what she said to you on the boat. Now that you aren't any use to her as a potential blackmail victim, she'll kill you. The woman is crazy—don't think she'll spare you."

Steve shifted uneasily, and the color drained from his face. "She'll have to catch me first," he said with forced bravado. "And I can run faster than she can."

Maddie shrugged her shoulders and said offhandedly, "Well, good luck."

Sounds of helicopters could still be heard, and Edena stood in the cave opening, staring at the sky, muttering angrily.

After several minutes, she came to stand over Steve and Maddie. "My cell phone won't work from this point. I've got a kinsman living down the mountain a ways. I'm going down there to see what's going on. If they're hunting for us, it may be on television."

Motioning to Maddie, she said, "Tie her up. She's smarter than you are, and she's liable to give you the slip. I want to be sure she's still here when I get back."

Wearily, Steve took some ropes out of his backpack and crawled toward Maddie. She was too tired to resist, so she crossed her hands behind her. She was aware that he didn't fasten her bonds as tightly as they'd been the night before.

"Gag her, now."

"Is that necessary? With this cave covering us, no one would hear her if she did call out."

"I ain't taking any chance on her being rescued. Put the gag on her."

Anger crossed Steve's face, but he put the gag in Maddie's mouth. She looked up and saw Edena hovering over Steve, a large rock in her hand. Perhaps the expression in her eyes warned him because he swung around, but he was too late. Edena struck him on the side of his head and Steve fell across Maddie's knees.

Laughing like a maniac, Edena pulled him away from Maddie, picked up some more rope and tied his hands and his feet. Taking a large flashlight out of her pack, she sniggered and said, "Don't go anywhere."

Moving fast for a big woman, she disappeared out of the cave in an instant.

Steve apparently wasn't dead, or she wouldn't have tied him, but he looked lifeless. If she expected to live to see another day, Maddie knew she had to leave this cave before the woman returned. She pulled on her hands, which Steve had tied loosely. Ignoring the pain in her wrists, and perspiring with the effort, she pulled and tugged on the ropes. She had no idea how much time had passed before she felt the ropes give a little. By that time, her wrists were bleeding, which in spite of the pain turned out to be a good thing, because when her wrists were wet with her own blood, it was easier to slip her arms out of the ropes.

Once her hands were freed, she quickly untied her feet and crawled to Steve's still body. He *was* breathing, and Maddie rummaged in his backpack and brought out another bottle of water. She drizzled it over his face until he opened his eyes. Maddie found a knife in the pack, too, and cut the ropes from his hands and feet.

She sloshed more water in his face. Holding his head, he sat up. "What happened?" he asked, still dazed.

"I got out of the ropes that you tied loosely. I'm leaving before Edena comes back."

Steve looked at her queerly. "You actually took time to save me after the way I've treated you?"

Without answering, Maddie searched Edena's pack. She pulled out a loaf of bread, some cheese and two bottles of water.

"I can't go far tonight, but I want to be well away from this cave before daylight. You can do what you want to."

Stuffing his belongings in the pack, Steve stood. "Where do you want to go?"

"To the place of refuge at the national park. I figure if I can get there, she'll be afraid to come after me. I'll stay there until someone rescues me."

"I'll go in the opposite direction. I've got a friend

at Kona, who'll help me. I have enough money to buy a one-way ticket to Japan. If Edena reports that I was involved in that theft at the Navy Department, I won't be safe in Hawaii. You can come with me to Kona."

"It's safer if we travel separately. She can't follow both of us."

He reached out his hand and Maddie took it. "You're an exceptional woman, Maddie. I hope you can escape this madwoman and that you and Linc have a happy marriage."

"I'm sorry you were involved in the crime."

He shrugged his shoulders. "That's what happens when you're too lazy to work."

He followed her out of the cave and handed her his flashlight. "There'll be a moon tonight, and I can travel better without a light than you can. Let me show you the best way to get to Pu'uhonua." He pointed to a light far below them. "That Coast Guard light is close to the park. If you keep it in sight, you won't lose your way. Good luck."

"Thanks, Steve. You, too."

She listened to Steve's fading footsteps for only a few minutes. Taking a deep breath, Maddie plunged into the darkness.

Too emotionally spent to go to the office, Linc went home to tell Roselina what had happened.

"Oh, Mr. Linc. That poor little thing. So much has happened to her. What can we do?"

"I've got the Honolulu police searching, as well

as Ed Blake. All I can do is sit beside the telephone and listen for some good news."

It was six o'clock when Claudia Warren telephoned him.

"I think we've got something, Mr. Carey, but I don't know if it's good or bad news."

Linc gripped the telephone tightly as he waited, holding his breath, to hear her report. Roselina hovered over his shoulder.

"A Coast Guard cutter picked up a suitcase floating near Kealakekua Bay. There was a rope on the suitcase as if someone had tried to sink it. They opened the case and found Madison Horton's name on several items."

"That sounds like she was taken to the island of Hawaii."

"That's the ancestral home of the Sanale family," Warren said. "We've also learned that two people, a man and a woman, loaded a long object in a motorboat and took off from Waikiki Beach early this morning. That bundle could have been Miss Horton."

This information frightened Linc. If it was Maddie, was she dead or alive? Had he finally found the one woman in the world for him, only to lose her?

"The police and the Coast Guard have been patrolling Hawaii in helicopters this afternoon. We'll start again at first light."

"I feel so useless, sitting here, waiting. What can I do?"

"Why not go to Hawaii tomorrow morning? It

seems likely that's where Miss Horton is, and you'll be close by when we pick her up." Warren gave him her mobile phone number. "Several members from our department are going, too, so you can stay in touch with me. I'll keep you posted on any progress we have."

Roselina wrung her hands when he told her about the floating suitcase.

"I only pray that they didn't dump Miss Maddie in the ocean, too."

As the same fear haunted Linc, he couldn't console her. Wiping her eyes, Roselina went into the kitchen, and Linc heard her praying. His mind was so numb, he couldn't pray, so it was a relief to know that Roselina was interceding on Maddie's behalf.

Ed Blake called soon afterward to report that he'd checked the airport, and that Maddie hadn't gone home. She'd had a reservation, but she hadn't shown up at the airport.

Linc told Ed the information he had. "Do you want to fly with me to Kona tomorrow? You might come in handy."

"Sure, buddy," Blake said. "As long as you're picking up the tab, I'll go wherever you want me to."

Knowing that Stella Oliver would be concerned about Maddie, Linc called her. The woman's voice sounded weary when she answered.

"This is Linc Carey."

"I'm so glad you called. I've been worried about Maddie. What have you learned?"

"Not a whole lot, unfortunately. But I did find

Maddie's ring in her room at the shelter. Knowing she wouldn't have gone away without it, I notified the police of her disappearance." He explained what he'd learned. "I'm going to Hawaii tomorrow to be close if they find her. How have things turned out for you?"

"The police have finally gone, but I'm afraid we aren't finished with them. They think the child was murdered because of what she knew about drug dealers in the area. One of the local policemen, related to the Sanales, has been put on an indefinite leave. There's an investigation to see if he opened the door to let someone in the night Maddie was taken. He isn't talking, but he's a suspect. I'm so sorry. I thought she was safe here."

"Don't blame yourself. The Sanales were determined to get her. I couldn't protect her, either. Now my main concern is to find her safe and unharmed. Pray for her, Stella."

SEVENTEEN

The moon moved in and out of the clouds enabling Maddie to keep the Coast Guard light in view. She walked carefully, favoring her aching feet, and most of the time she could see the path without turning on the flashlight. When the moon disappeared behind a cloud, she groped her way along, holding on to rocks and bushes to keep from plunging down a steep incline. She hadn't walked more than a half hour before her hands were burning from contact with the ragged rocks.

She knew immediately when Edena returned and discovered her prisoners were gone. An anguished scream rang across the mountains, and either Edena shouted continually, or the sound echoed through the mountain valleys. Maddie had heard lots of echoing in the hills of her native state, but she didn't know whether that also happened in Hawaii.

Terrified of the woman, Maddie started running, stumbled over a rock and rolled downward until she slammed against a tree so hard she gasped for breath.

A crashing through the underbrush behind her indicated that Edena was following her. Maddie crawled away from the trail and hid behind a large boulder. She peered around the corner of the rock as Edena, ranting and raging like a maniac, plunged downhill, not bothering to keep to the trail.

Breathlessly, she monitored the woman's retreating footsteps. Maddie knew she couldn't continue in that direction, but if she changed course, she'd lose the beacon of the Coast Guard light. It had taken several hours to climb the hill, but it would take less time to go down. Still, if she couldn't see the light, she could quickly lose her bearings.

Feeling safe for the moment, Maddie leaned against the rock, hoping a little rest would stop the pounding of her heart. Would she be wiser to wait until morning to continue? She would be less likely to fall and sustain a serious injury in daylight. Edena would see her more easily, too, but on the other hand, she could see Edena and keep out of her way.

From Edena's wailing, which she could still hear plainly, it was evident that the woman was heading in the opposite direction of Maddie's destination. She had probably picked up Steve's trail, thinking that Maddie and Steve were together.

Maddie wondered momentarily how Steve was faring. She was surprised at how kind he'd been to her. She'd never given much thought to Steve one way or another. She'd only met him a few times, and she'd always thought he was a weakling, depending upon his sister. His involvement in the theft for which the Sanale brothers had been imprisoned would land him in prison if he were caught. She actually found herself hoping he could flee to Japan. She'd helped him by untying him and giving him a chance to escape, and she hoped she wouldn't have to tell the authorities anything about his past.

When the sounds of Edena's wailing faded completely, Maddie drank some water, turned on the flashlight, and walked toward the coast. She stumbled into a barnyard beside a small dwelling. A dog lunged in her direction, barking and snarling at her. Maddie jumped backward and evaded the dog, relieved to know that he was tied. A light came on in the house, and she ran quickly back the way she'd come. They might be the relatives Edena had gone to find. In any case, the barking dog could alert Edena to her whereabouts.

Maddie rushed on until she came to a steep incline that she couldn't walk down. She didn't have a watch, and she had no idea what time it was, but she decided to wait until daylight. Using the light again, she located a small cave and crawled into it, thankful that she didn't have to worry about snakes in Hawaii.

Maddie wished for a Bible, but she supposed the one Miss Caroline had given her when she left VOH was at the bottom of the Pacific with her other possessions. Leaning against the damp wall of the cave, Maddie wondered why she wasn't more afraid than she was. Miss Caroline spent hours each night praying for the current and former residents of VOH. Considering the time difference, Miss Caroline had finished her nightly prayers, but Maddie had no doubt that her mentor had talked to God about her situation. By now Linc would know she'd been kidnapped, and he and Roselina would be praying, too.

As she waited for sleep to come, Maddie remembered that David, a Hebrew king mentioned in the Old Testament, had been trapped in a cave by his enemies. God had delivered David from the wrath of King Saul. David had written several of his psalms of worship and praise when he'd been running from his enemies. At one time his enemies had surrounded his house, and he'd prayed for God to deliver him from the ones who'd risen up against him. David had faith that God would deliver him, and Maddie remembered the words he'd written.

For You are my fortress, my refuge in times of trouble. O my Strength, I sing praise to You; You, O God, are my fortress, my loving God.

God, I do praise You tonight for delivering me from my enemy. I feel evil closing around me, but there's a way out of my predicament. I may not know the way, but You do. God, I pray for Linc tonight. In spite of our angry words to each other, I believe he loves me, and he'll be really worried about me. Please bring us together again as soon as possible if it's Your will.

It was still dark when Maddie woke up, and she wondered anxiously what time it was. The moon was no longer shining, so that could mean it was almost daylight. She took the bread and cheese from the pack Steve had strapped on her back, ate about half of it, and started on her last bottle of water.

A crowing rooster alerted Maddie, indicating that daylight was imminent. It also told Maddie she was still too close to that little farmstead. Slowly, light filtered around her, and she felt like crying when she noticed that a heavy fog covered the mountain. She couldn't see more than ten feet in any direction. What could she do? Which direction should she go? She had to make some move, and she walked cautiously along the cliff area until she saw a narrow path going downward. She had no idea in which direction she was going. She knew it would eventually lead to the coast, but it might be in the opposite direction from the park.

As the sky lightened, she surmised that the sun was shining, but still she couldn't see. She became aware that helicopters were flying around the island. She heard a plane fly overhead, which sounded like the motor of Linc's, but for all she knew, dozens of airplanes might have the same sound.

When the fog finally lifted, Maddie was still a long way from the water, but there was a small town a few miles below her. If she went there, she could probably get some help, but she might also encounter Edena. She chose to stay out of sight as much as possible, but when a helicopter flew overhead, she took off her shirt, stepped out into the open and waved it back and forth. She thought the pilot had seen her because he circled her position two times before he flew away. She knew there wasn't any place a helicopter could land on this mountain, so she shrugged into her shirt and hurried on. She judged she was only a mile from the coast when she turned and saw Edena behind her. Maddie didn't think Edena had seen her, however, for she was looking at the ground, perhaps trying to find Maddie's tracks.

Maddie had no time to waste, and keeping undercover as much as she could, she ran downward. Soon she saw Hōnaunau Park below her with the reconstructed place of refuge on its little peninsula. She ran out on the pebbly beach and stopped in dismay. When she and Linc had been here, it must have been low tide, for there had been very little water in the inlet. Now several feet of water stood between her and safety.

She recalled the day she'd envisioned an ancient prisoner who had run down the steep hill seeking refuge. She'd thought how discouraged he would have been if he couldn't cross the water. She could empathize with the hunted man now. Could she possibly swim through that water?

Hearing calls from the other side of the inlet, she saw two men. One of them was Linc. "I'm coming after you," he called. He jumped into the water and started swimming toward her.

Hearing a shout behind her, Maddie looked over

her shoulder. Edena was no more than thirty feet away, stumbling along the path. Maddie had never swum in the ocean, and as tired as she was, she didn't know if she was able to swim, but she wouldn't stand here and wait for Edena to capture her.

She threw away the backpack and rushed into the water. The high waves swirling around her legs threw her off balance, and she fell headfirst into the water. She surfaced and saw Linc's graceful strokes as he swam toward her. Her strength was about spent, but she kept the place of refuge in view between strokes. Every minute she expected Edena to come up behind her until she remembered the woman's statement that she didn't know how to swim.

Once a wave turned Maddie over, and she floundered in the strong current. When she surfaced, she blinked the water from her eyes and located Linc not far away.

They met midway. "Hold on to me," Linc said, "and let me tow you to shore. We'll make it."

The waves of the incoming tide buoyed them toward shore. When Linc's feet touched bottom, he put his arm around Maddie and pulled her to safety. He slumped down on the beach and Maddie collapsed beside him as they struggled to breathe.

Several state policemen surrounded them, and Maddie knew she was safe at last. She leaned on an elbow, looked across the water and saw Edena disappearing into the bushes, heading back up the hill.

One of the cops said, "We'll get her. She can't get

very far. We'll radio police in Kona and Hilo to help us. Are you all right, ma'am?"

She nodded. Detective Warren knelt beside her.

Taking stock of Maddie's torn clothing, her scratched arms and legs, and her bedraggled appearance, Warren said, "You may be all right, but you're going to the hospital. Soon enough to talk about your experiences later. We have an ambulance standing by."

Two orderlies came with a gurney, and when they took hold of Maddie's arm to help her to stand, she collapsed. Linc crawled to her side.

"Maddie!" he cried. He looked up at Claudia Warren, who felt the pulse in Maddie's neck and wrist.

"She's all right. I suspect shock and exhaustion caused her to faint. We'll take her to the hospital in Kona. You can follow in your car."

Whether from shock or fatigue, Maddie slept for eighteen hours. Linc refused to leave her. His anger was kindled when he saw the bruise on her fair skin where she'd been hit. Her wrists were bandaged, but he'd seen the abrasions on her arms when she'd been rescued.

He hovered over her bed, caressing her hands until a nurse said, "You'll have to go out of the room if you don't leave her alone. The woman is worn out. She needs to rest." With a sympathetic smile, she patted him on the shoulder, saying, "Will you behave?"

"Yes," he said reluctantly, backing away from the bed.

"Then sit in that chair by the window and take a nap. You look as bad as she does, and we don't want you for a patient."

Linc did as the nurse said, and Maddie woke up before he did. She had an IV in her arm, and wires strung all over her body. She lay motionless, not knowing if she should, or could, move. She quietly watched the even rise and fall of Linc's chest. His head leaned against the back of the chair. He'd taken off his shoes and propped his feet on a waste-paper can. A stubble of beard blackened his face and his hair was tousled, as if he'd been frantically threading it with his fingers. A blanket covered his body.

The door opened, and a nurse peered into the room. When Maddie smiled at her and put her finger to her lips in a bid for silence, the nurse glanced toward Linc. She moved quietly to Maddie's bed, took her pulse and temperature, and checked her blood pressure.

"How are you feeling?" she said softly.

"Like I've been in a fight with a wildcat. My hands and feet burn, and I'm sore all over. My lips are swollen. Other than that I'm in good shape," she added with a grimace.

"Mr. Carey might need his sleep," the nurse said, "but he's been waiting for hours to talk to you. He won't forgive me if I don't let him know you're awake."

She walked to the window, pulled the blinds and

drapes aside. Linc stirred, yawned, apparently realized where he was, and his eyes darted toward Maddie's bed. He jumped out of the chair and hurried to her in his stocking feet.

"How are you?" he said anxiously.

"Alive! That's all that matters."

He leaned toward her, and his lips grazed hers tenderly. "I've lived through torment the last few days, fearing I'd never see you again. I don't know how I'd have lived without you." He turned to the nurse. "When can I take her home?"

"Her doctor will have to decide that, but I imagine she'll have to stay for another day, at least." She smoothed the pillows under Maddie's head, asking, "Are you hungry?"

"I don't know. I'm thirsty, though."

"I'll order some juice and fruit for you. And a tray for you, Mr. Carey, so you eat with her."

When the nurse left, Linc caressed Maddie's face with a tender hand. "It was the Sanales who kidnapped you, I guess."

"Only *one* Sanale, who happens to be a woman. Her brother, Kamu, died from a wound he received when he broke out of prison. Edena took it on herself to avenge the deaths of all the male members of her family."

"But the police thought that two people kidnapped you."

She looked at him strangely, "And you don't know who the man was?"

He stared at her, shaking his head.

"Steve Kingsbury."

He staggered a little and pulled a chair close to the bed. "But why?"

"He was involved in the theft that the Sanales were imprisoned for. They didn't betray him, for they thought when they got out of prison, they could blackmail him. Edena was mad because Steve didn't amount to much and didn't have anything to pay them. She forced him to help her do away with me or she'd report him to the police."

"So that's why Ahonui wanted me to send you home. She was trying to protect you. I guess I owe her an apology."

"I feel bad about Steve. He obviously didn't want to harm me."

"How did they get you? Why did you leave your room?"

"Steve told me you'd had a plane accident. That you were in the hospital, asking for me, and you'd told him where I was."

"That isn't true."

"I know that now. As soon as I let him in the room, they gave me a shot that put me out. How did you know where I was?"

"Edena had left a note, supposedly from you, saying that you were going home. It was written on a computer, but the words didn't sound like you. I couldn't believe you'd leave in the middle of the night, and when I was looking around the room, I found your opal ring under the pillow. I knew then that you hadn't left voluntarily."

"I'm glad I have that left, anyway. Edena tied rocks around my suitcases and pitched them in the ocean."

"But one of them didn't sink. That's how we found you so quickly. The Coast Guard picked up the suitcase, opened it and there were things inside that identified you. The police called me."

An aide came in with their food, and Linc ate heartily as Maddie continued to explain. The orange juice stung her bruised lips and she sipped it cautiously.

"I can't believe Steve would be involved in all of this," Linc said. "Of course, he never has been very ambitious—I've suspected for a long time that Ahonui financed him. And I suppose when he helped the Sanales steal from the Navy Department, he thought it was an easy way to turn a buck."

"I hope I won't have to lead the police to him, for he tried to make the ordeal as easy as possible for me."

She told him how Edena had tied up both of them, and when she'd convinced Steve that the woman intended to kill him, too, he decided to leave Hawaii. "I wanted to get away from Edena as soon as possible, so he shared some of the food with me and pointed me in the quickest route to the coast. He went in another direction, but I hope I won't have to tell the police where."

"You can do as you wish, but I wouldn't withhold information from the police. If Steve is caught and punished, he brought all of this on himself."

The nurse came in again. "Detective Warren wants to talk to you now. Are you up to it?"

"I guess so," Maddie said. "I might as well get it over with."

EIGHTEEN

The few times Maddie had met the detective, she had been impressed by her kindness and efficiency. She was glad she could talk to her rather than a stranger.

"I don't want to tire you, Miss Horton," Warren said, "so when you've had enough, tell me, and we'll continue at another time."

"I don't know where to start," Maddie said, and she looked toward Linc. Seeing the fear and uncertainty in her eyes, he stood by her bed and held her right hand carefully so as not to dislodge the IV.

She curled her fingers around his, and with a light smile, she said, "Both of you had better sit down—this may take an hour or so."

Linc pulled the chair he'd slept in toward the bed for Warren. He perched on the edge of the bed beside Maddie. The nurse on duty entered the room and stood at the foot of the bed.

"Doctor's orders," she said with a smile. "I'm to see that you don't overly stress our patient."

"I'd only been in Hawaii a few days when I was

sure that someone was stalking me," Maddie started. "Sometimes it was a man, other times, I thought it was a woman, but they looked alike. I know now that I was shadowed by Kamu Sanale's twin sister, Edena. Sometimes she dressed as a man."

She explained to Warren, as she had to Linc, how she had been tricked into leaving her room and had been brought to Hawaii. Her hands moistened, and she often closed her eyes and rubbed her head, when she explained how Edena had destroyed her luggage and how she'd been gagged and forced to climb the mountain. The nurse stepped to her side and checked her pulse.

At that point, Warren asked, "Who was Edena's accomplice?"

Maddie swallowed. "I really hate to tell you this, for he was good to me and helped me escape from Edena, but I know I must." She slanted an enquiring look at Linc, and he encouraged her with a smile.

"Go ahead," he said.

"It was Steve Kingsbury, the brother of Linc's office assistant. I'd seen him a few times. Edena called him Tivini."

"That's the Hawaiian name for Steven. We know that Kingsbury was involved with the Sanale family, but we don't know why." She fixed Maddie with her piercing eyes. "Do you know?"

Maddie nodded affirmatively.

"I overheard them talking in the boat before they left Waikiki Beach. Steve had been their accomplice in the theft from the Navy Department, but he wasn't suspected. The Sanales didn't report him, but Edena indicated that her brothers had expected to blackmail him for their livelihood when they got out of prison. I'm sure that she meant to kill Steve as well as myself. But when she made Steve tie me up, he left the ropes loose enough on my wrists that I freed myself and then freed him. We went in different directions as we escaped. Steve said that would confuse Edena. I suppose she thought we were together, for she came plunging down the mountain after me not very long after we escaped."

"Perhaps I shouldn't ask," Linc said, "but have you caught them yet?"

"Edena wasn't hard to find. When she saw that Miss Horton was safe, she went back to the burial cave. We found her there. She'd stabbed herself to death."

Maddie shuddered and covered her face.

"Knowing what I do about their religion," Warren continued, "I assume she reasoned that since *you* escaped, she'd offer her own life in recompense for the death of her family members."

"And Kingsbury?" Linc asked. Although he had been annoyed at Ahonui for the past month, he knew she loved her brother.

"We haven't found him yet, but he's not likely to escape. We have cops patrolling the southern end of this island in helicopters, cruisers, patrol boats and even on foot. I only hope we can catch him."

Maddie nodded emphatic agreement, but the gesture made her neck hurt. She frowned.

Warren stood. "I see you've had enough for one day, Miss Horton. I'm sorry your visit to Hawaii has been so traumatic. I pray that the rest of your time here will be more pleasant. Thanks for your help. The Coast Guard has the piece of luggage they discovered. I understand there was some water damage, but not everything was ruined. Where can I have them deliver it to you?"

"At my house," Linc said quickly. "There isn't any reason for her to return to Open Arms Shelter now."

Warren shook hands with Linc, and he said, "I appreciate your dedication to this case." With a smile, he added, "I hope I won't have to bother you again for a *long* time."

"It's all in a day's work for me," Warren said.

When they were alone, Linc said, "It's all over now, sweetheart. Try to put it behind you."

"God forgive me, if this is the wrong attitude," Maddie said, "but I can't help but be glad that Edena is dead. I don't think I'd ever feel safe again if she was still living with that intense hatred."

"As far as I know, she's the end of that branch of the Sanale family. Neither she nor her siblings ever married. The extended family probably believes that her suicide atoned for the death of her father and brothers."

The door opened and the doctor entered.

"Miss Horton, all of your vital signs are good, so I don't see any reason you can't be discharged. But I'd advise you to take it easy for several days. When are you scheduled to return to the mainland?"

"I had a reservation for two days ago. I'll have to reschedule."

"We'll talk about that later on," Linc said quickly.

"Delay your departure for a week or so," the doctor said.

"My insurance cards were in my purse, and I suppose Edena destroyed all of those. I can get them reissued, but it will take a little time."

"I'll take care of the hospital bill," Linc said. "But I think your purse was in the suitcase the Coast Guard recovered. If so, maybe your personal papers will be all right."

The clothes Maddie had worn to the hospital were torn and useless, so Linc asked one of the hospital employees to buy two sets of clothes for her.

"I don't want you to buy my clothes. If my purse is okay, I'll have the money to buy some things."

"Okay, okay," Linc said. "You can pay me back when you get your purse. In a few days after you're feeling better, Roselina can take you shopping."

The woman purchased two tops, a pair of slacks, a pair of capris, underwear and some sandals. While Linc was in the office taking care of her bill, the nurse helped Maddie shower and dress. Every part of her body was sore to the touch, and she was weak enough that she didn't protest when the nurse put her in a wheelchair and took her to Linc's car.

An attendant at the airport helped Linc load her into the plane, and they headed for Oahu.

Linc had never talked much when he piloted the plane, but he seemed more quiet than usual today. Maddie didn't feel like talking, either, and she leaned back, often with her eyes closed, wondering what the next step in their relationship would be.

The trauma of her abduction and the stress of the past few days had seemed to wipe out the bitterness of their last time together. But she couldn't presume on Linc's kindness. He would have looked out for her and taken care of her needs either way—whether he felt like a father, or if he loved her as an adult.

If he didn't say anything, as soon as she felt up to the trip, she had no choice except to return home.

The Pacific had never seemed more beautiful and majestic to Maddie. Waikiki Beach gleamed in the sun as Linc crossed it on his way to landing.

"God, thank you for protecting me and bringing me back here safely," Maddie prayed aloud and Linc added a fervent, *"Amen."*

Linc had called Roselina from the airport, and she stood on the veranda waiting for them. She ran toward the car and was panting when she opened the door. Tears rolled down her plump cheeks. She ran her hands over Maddie's face and arms, as if to assure herself that Maddie really had returned.

"Welcome home, Miss Maddie. Welcome home.

I've prayed so much for you that I've worn calluses on my knees. God's good to bring you back to us."

"God is good all the time, Roselina. Even if my life had been taken, God is good."

"Oh, I know," Roselina said. "But Mr. Linc and I weren't ready to give you up, honey."

Linc tapped Roselina on the shoulder. "Let's get our invalid in the house, so you can start pampering her."

He took Maddie's arm, and when she winced from standing on her sore feet in a new pair of shoes, Linc whipped her up in his arms.

"Oh, put me down," she protested. "I can walk."

Nuzzling her soft, fragrant hair, he said, "But I can carry you, too."

As he passed through the front door, he said, giving Maddie a hint of what was to come, "I have to carry you over the threshold sometime."

She lowered her eyes from his whimsical expression, unwilling to dwell on the implication of his words when she wasn't feeling up to par. She knew she wasn't yet over her experience when her body started trembling, and she couldn't stop it.

Linc lowered her slowly to her feet, and she dropped wearily into a chair.

"This won't do," Linc said in alarm. "You need to rest. Roselina, I'll carry her upstairs and you can put her to bed. The doctor said she needed a few days of bed rest."

Too weary to protest, Maddie welcomed his strong arms as he again lifted her and walked easily upstairs.

She closed her eyes to hold back the tears of frustration and weakness. She wanted to be strong for Linc's sake, but she was too tired to worry about it.

Roselina hurried into the bedroom and had the covers laid back by the time Linc walked into the room. He laid Maddie on the bed and took off her sandals.

"I think all of her clothes have been destroyed, but one of the nurses bought a few things for her. Also, I have some medication for her. I'll bring them and leave her in your care."

When Roselina didn't find a gown in the bag of clothes, she rustled into her room and brought back a soft, cotton gown. She helped Maddie remove her clothes, and she slipped on the gown, which was much too large for Maddie. All the time she worked with her, Roselina patted Maddie and whispered to her consolingly as she would have a child. It had been so long since anyone had babied Maddie that she liked it. Perhaps it wouldn't be so bad if Linc would treat her like a child sometimes. After Roselina gave her a sedative, Maddie started to feel sleepy. She was still alert enough to know that she didn't want him to treat her like a child *all* of the time.

Maddie slept through most of three days. Either Roselina or Linc were in the room every time she wakened. They fed her, turned her in the bed and Roselina took care of her personal needs. When she tried to talk to them, she dropped off to sleep.

On the fourth day, Maddie woke up and felt

normal again. She was alone in the room, and she examined the scratches and wounds on her arms, checked the blisters on her feet to find they were healing. She noticed that she had on a new gown that fit her. A new robe lay across the foot of the bed, and she decided that Roselina had been shopping.

She swung her feet out of bed, noticing that some of her muscles were still sore, but she'd stayed in bed too long. It was only six in the morning by the bedside clock, so Linc and Roselina were probably still asleep. She got up, put on her robe and walked to the window, opened it and stepped out on the balcony. The breeze from the ocean graced her body, and a sliver of moon hovered behind the palm trees on the beach.

She sat in a chair and gloried in the unbelievable beauty and serenity of the place. Had Linc been hinting of marriage when he'd made the comment about carrying her over the threshold? If he asked her to marry him, would she be willing to give up the way of life she'd always known to move to Hawaii? Since Linc's business was here, there would be no other way.

She was suddenly conscious that she wasn't alone and she turned. Linc stood behind her.

"And what are you doing out of bed?" he said in mock severity.

"I've had enough sleep. How long have I been here?"

"Three days. Do you *really* feel like getting up?"

He knelt by her side and lifted her hand.

"I actually feel better than I have for a month," she said. "I want to get dressed today. Have you been to work since I've been here?"

"No, but I'll go today if you're feeling all right. There are several matters that I need to look into."

"Have you been in contact with the police?"

"A few times. Detective Warren brought your suitcase. I put it in the closet. The police had gone through everything for fingerprints and any evidence. You have a few clothes in it, and your cosmetics and jewelry. Your purse was inside, too. Roselina bought a few things for you to wear, but she'll take you shopping when you feel up to it."

"Which isn't today," Maddie said as she stood. "My legs still feel a little wobbly, but I would like to go downstairs."

"You haven't had much to eat—that's one reason you're weak. You'd take a few bites and go back to sleep. It was the medication doing that, but we only had pills for three days, so you should be more alert now."

"I'll take a shower, dress and come down for breakfast."

"Do you need Roselina's help?"

"No, I'm weak, but I don't feel dizzy. I'll be all right."

When Linc returned from work, Maddie was seated on the patio watching the ocean. She looked better, and he couldn't delay longer in talking to her about the future.

"I've listened to the television news today. I didn't hear anything about our case," she said.

"There was quite a lot for a day or two, telling about your capture and escape, as well as Edena's death. The navy apparently withheld information about Steve, but they've announced that the investigation into your father's death has been closed. The reporters have learned that the police are still looking for more leads in your kidnapping, but they haven't named Steve, either. I didn't mention his name to Ahonui today, but she's obviously worried."

"He told me he planned to leave Hawaii for good, so he may be gone by now."

"If he's gone, Ahonui will follow him, and I'll lose a good secretary. But perhaps it will be just as well. Things are tense between us now, and I'm not sure I can trust her. I keep wondering if she knew about your abduction and didn't tell me."

After dinner, Maddie said, "Let's go to the beach."

"Are you sure you're able to walk that far?" Linc asked anxiously.

"I feel stronger now than when I got up this morning."

"I'll take the chairs and we can rest a while before we come back."

His voice sounded weary, and she commented on the lines of fatigue around his eyes.

"I've had a pretty rough week, too," he said. "Not knowing where you were or what was happening to

you was the worst experience of my life. Now that
I know you're getting better, I'll soon be up to par."

He put the chairs close together, and they held
hands, silently watching the incoming tide. A pair
of brown sandpipers with yellow legs wandered
along the beach.

After a long sigh, Maddie said, "I've never apologized to you for the way I acted when you took me to
dinner that night. I was way out of line in what I said."

He squeezed her hand tighter. "I shouldn't have
lost my temper, either, but you were right, of course.
For my own peace of mind, I'd forced myself to
consider you as a child. I thought we were too far
apart in age for me to think of you any other way. I'd
heard of too many May-December marriages failing.
I felt guilty to think about you the way I did. But
when you were abducted, and I thought I'd lost you
forever, I made up my mind to speak when we were
reunited."

A small enchanted smile touched her lips, and
her eyes brightened with pleasure. He was encouraged to continue.

"I fell for you when I first saw you in the
airport. I've never believed in love at first sight, but
that's what happened to me. You looked so childlike and innocent, I decided to keep my feelings
to myself. But I do love you, Maddie, and I want
to marry you. Can you be happy living in Hawaii
as my wife?"

"I've tried to sort out my feelings today, so I could

answer you if you asked me. Linc, I've loved you since I was a child. I found a picture of you in Daddy's belongings, and I've kept it on my dresser, or somewhere in sight, for years. I have it in my purse even now. When I saw you again, it didn't take long for that childish love to become an adult love. But to answer your question—I'll be happy as your wife, no matter where we live."

Linc's reaction to that statement kept them so busy for the next few minutes that they weren't able to talk. But finally Linc released her.

"Although I think you should finish your college degree, which you can do here in Hawaii, I don't want to wait two more years to get married. If you're willing to marry right away, you wouldn't have to take on the duties of the house. Roselina will stay with us, I'm sure, for a few years. Her kids want her to come to live with them in California, but she won't do that right away, if at all. I don't necessarily want you to work, but I want you to be prepared for a profession if anything should happen to me. I'd like for us to have a family, but that's up to you."

"I will finish college for security reasons, but I like the idea of having a family, and being a stay-at-home mom."

"We can make those decisions as the months move along. But right now, let's set the day for the wedding. Would a month from today be too soon?"

"That sounds perfect."

"Where shall we go for the wedding?"

"Where else but to the Wedding Grotto!" she said, with mischief in her eye. "When we were there, I dared to dream that it might be the site for our wedding."

"And a honeymoon?"

"Let's go to Maui. Ailina, my roommate at the shelter, told me it was the best of the islands."

They continued to make plans as night settled along the ocean. The romance and mystery of Hawaii that had called thousands of lovers to its shores hovered around them. The waning moon, long past its zenith, sent a ray of light on the two heads very close together. As darkness completely fell, Linc cradled his willing companion in his arms. Maddie put her arms around his neck, lifted her lips to his, convincing him without a doubt that she wasn't too young for him to marry.

Dear Reader,

I'm finishing this book during the Christmas season, and my mind has often turned to the birth of the Christ Child. In our home, Christmas is irrevocably tied to the celebration of the coming of Jesus with our church family. For years, my husband and I have been involved in the production of the annual cantata. And we customarily give a dinner of appreciation for all the cast members, sometimes numbering between forty and fifty people. Up until the past two years, we've entertained in our own home, preparing a sit-down dinner for them. Now the lack of time and the addition of years make it more convenient to have the dinner catered and served in our church annex.

And since this book's setting is Hawaii, as I've put the finishing touches on the book I've thought often of our vacation in Hawaii, which inspired me to do a novel in that setting. When my husband and I went to the fiftieth state in 2003, it was also the fiftieth state we'd toured. Not only did that vacation count as the last of the states to be visited, it was also a time of relaxation and fellowship with a group of Christians from our state.

As you read this book, I pray that your mind will focus on the real meaning of Christmas, and that the Christ Child will find lodging in your heart.

To comment on the book, please e-mail me at irenebrand@zoomnet.net, or by snail mail, P.O. Box 2770, Southside, WV 25187.

Irene B. Brand

QUESTIONS FOR DISCUSSION

1. Maddie Horton is ten and Linc Carey is twenty-one when they first meet. Do you think it's realistic to believe that Maddie would have been so impressed by Linc at the age of ten that she would "carry the torch" for him throughout her teen years?

2. When Linc finally meets the grown-up Maddie, he falls in love. He has always remembered Maddie as a cute little girl, but suddenly his feelings change. Do you believe in love at first sight? Give examples.

3. Although Maddie has physically developed into a woman, the reader senses that behind her beautiful facade there is emotional and mental insecurity. How much did the loss of her parents contribute to this insecurity? How valuable is a stable home environment to the emotional maturation of a child?

4. Do you believe that Maddie's years at the Valley of Hope gave her the courage to face the future on her own? Would you have continued to rely on advice from Miss Caroline, as Maddie did? Is it important for everyone to have a mentor to keep them on the right track in making decisions? If you have or have had a mentor such as Miss Caroline, share what help this person gave you.

5. When Maddie escapes from Edena, the Hawaiian woman who intended to kill her, she spends the night alone on the mountain. She remembers the times when David, the Old Testament king, had turned to God for help when he was running from his enemies. Consider the following references from the Psalms when David spoke of God as his Rock and Fortress. Discuss

if these words have also encouraged you through difficult times. Psalms 18:2; 31:3; 71:3; 91:2; 144:2

6. Do you agree with Linc that eleven years is too much of an age difference for Maddie and him to have a happy marriage? Do you think that he does treat her like a child? Are couples whose ages are very close more compatible than those whose ages vary widely?

7. Discuss Linc's recommitment to God when they visit The Place of Refuge. Consider Maddie's analogy that the ancient Hawaiian belief of finding a refuge from their enemies on the island is comparable to the refuge we can find when we seek shelter from God. Do you agree that this is a good comparison?

8. The relationship between Elizabeth Barrett Browning and her husband, Robert, is one of the world's most famous romances. Research the difficulties that kept the Brownings from marrying for several years. Compare their relationship to Maddie and Linc's by remembering that there was also an age difference between the Brownings. Elizabeth was born in 1806 and Robert in 1812, but that wasn't a deterrent to their love. Elizabeth's "Sonnet 43" is her most famous poem. With Robert in mind, Elizabeth started the poem "How do I love thee? Let me count the ways." Close your discussion by recounting the reasons Maddie and Linc love one another. Then think of the love of your life and why you love that person.

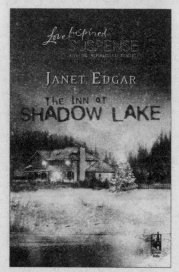

REQUEST YOUR FREE BOOKS!

2 FREE INSPIRATIONAL NOVELS
PLUS 2
FREE
MYSTERY GIFTS

Love Inspired.

YES! Please send me 2 FREE Love Inspired® novels and my 2 FREE mystery gifts. After receiving them, if I don't wish to receive any more books, I can return the shipping statement marked "cancel." If I don't cancel, I will receive 4 brand-new novels every month and be billed just $3.99 per book in the U.S., or $4.74 per book in Canada, plus 25¢ shipping and handling per book and applicable taxes, if any*. That's a savings of at least 20% off the cover price! I understand that accepting the 2 free books and gifts places me under no obligation to buy anything. I can always return a shipment and cancel at any time. Even if I never buy another book from Steeple Hill, the two free books and gifts are mine to keep forever.

113 IDN EF26   313 IDN EF27

Name	(PLEASE PRINT)	
Address		Apt.
City	State/Prov.	Zip/Postal Code

Signature (if under 18, a parent or guardian must sign)

Order online at www.LoveInspiredBooks.com

Or mail to Steeple Hill Reader Service™:

IN U.S.A.
P.O. Box 1867
Buffalo, NY
14240-1007

IN CANADA
P.O. Box 609
Fort Erie, Ontario
L2A 5X3

Not valid to current Love Inspired subscribers.

Want to try two free books from another series?
Call 1-800-873-8635 or visit www.morefreebooks.com

* Terms and prices subject to change without notice. NY residents add applicable sales tax. Canadian residents will be charged applicable provincial taxes and GST. This offer is limited to one order per household All orders subject to approval. Credit or debit balances in a customer's account(s) may be offset by any other outstanding balance owed by or to the customer. Please allow 4 to 6 weeks for delivery.

LIREG06

Love Inspired®

LASSO HER HEART

BY

ANNA SCHMIDT

After her fiancé's death, Bethany Taft didn't think happily-ever-after existed for her. Yet when her aunt got engaged at sixty, spending time with the groom's son, Cody Dillard, made her rethink her position. But it would take work for the handsome rancher to lasso Bethany's heart!

Available December 2006, wherever you buy books.

Steeple Hill®

Love Inspired
SUSPENSE

TITLES AVAILABLE NEXT MONTH

Don't miss these two stories in December

OUT OF THE DEPTHS by Valerie Hansen

Trudy Lynn Brown needed someone to help her get rid of the vandals threatening her campground. Cody Keringhoven fit the bill, yet how can the recently injured Cody find the strength to protect her with criminals determined to drive her away?

THE INN AT SHADOW LAKE by Janet Edgar

Special Agent Zachary Marshall had tracked a deadly terrorist ring to a secluded resort—right to a woman he'd once loved. He found himself falling for Julie Anderson all over again, but was she a cunning traitor...or an innocent victim of ruthless criminals?

LISCNM1106